MUSIC AND MURDER

A Benny Wright Story: Book 2

Dennis A Nehamen

Golden Poppy Publications
Los Angeles

I recall many years ago having a patient who was a top executive at a record company. He sought me out for my professional counsel not owing to music, but to murder. Who it was that had been eliminated did not matter, and he had no intent to disclose to me the identity of the unfortunate target of revenge and betrayal. He was aware that crime had been committed; his problem was that he was too frightened to report it. Sharing with me was his only relief from the enduring agony he was suffering. Music and Murder: He assured me that beneath the glitz and glamour of the celebrities entertaining the public was a world of hard nose business people, ones that didn't like it when things went against them. Trance Williams, known as Triple-XXX, and his buddy Brent Calhoun, performing under the name of Rough Diamond, found out the hard way.

Fortunately, not all souls aspiring for artistic fame and wealth wash up dead on to beaches of obscurity. Most graduate their fantasies of acclaim into the simple joy and wonder of creation, and in this way achieve satisfaction perhaps greater than those glorified for their contributions. This book is dedicated to the pursuits and projects of the unheralded and unacknowledged artists of the world—one might label them, the true survivors.

CHAPTER 1: BLOODY BAD LUCK...AGAIN

It was almost five in the afternoon. Fall had descended on our neighborhood in a most generous and gorgeous fashion. The signature pair of giant white ash trees canopying our home—lovebirds, a male and a female—had been dressed in a yellow color although there was a purple shading on the underside of the leaves that rained beams of sparkling light that were being sopped up by the moistness of the ground below.

I had just arrived home. Through the large bay window of our living room, I was admiring the dignity of these specimens that proudly distinguished my modest house. It was then that I noticed a vehicle come to a stop across the street. I vaguely recognized it as one I had seen many times before but didn't make the connection until the man driving hopped out. Then I understood why the car struck a tone of familiarity: it belonged to a young man I'd mentored with his career as a singer and performer, Trance Williams.

I noticed he vigilantly scanned every direction. Even from a distance, I could discern that he was agitated over something. He jogged across the asphalt street and then along the cement path leading to the porch of my home. I opened the door before he had the opportunity to knock. Trance stood staring at me. At first, he didn't say a word.

When he noticed my wife Jewel sitting reading a book, he waved to her and forced a smile before motioning to me that he preferred that I come outdoors where he could talk to me in private. The weather had made a dramatic turn during the previous week, another autumnal indicator. In fact, it was quite cold and I hadn't taken a coat with me.

"I'm sorry, Benny," Trance panted. "I needed to see you."

"Let's get into my car...it's a bit chilly for an old guy like me," I joked to relieve a tension, the source of which I had no idea.

Trance was usually a very cool, easy-going kid. In truth, I'd never witnessed him in a funk.

"Benny, I might be in some trouble," he stammered. "I don't want to get you involved...with all you've been through."

"Why don't you tell me what you're talking about and let's see if we can't figure out what to do?"

I thought he was going to educate me about the issue that was bothering him, when I heard a sound from outside my home. I glanced left. Jewel was calling me. I opened the window and she shouted that my friend, Simon, was on the phone. I told her to let him know I'd call back. In the interim, Trance appeared to reach an even greater level of angst. I noticed that he was breathing heavily and despite the temperature in my car, his underarms had produced sufficient moisture to change the color of his pale blue t-shirt to a foreboding deep oceanic tone.

Then he did what I was not expecting. He abruptly whipped open the passenger-door and jumped out.

"Benny, God Bless you. You've meant a lot to me. I'll never forget what you've done."

Then he made a quick dash back into his car.

"Trance, we can talk about it," I entreated as he leapt into the driver's seat and drove off at a speed inappropriate for a residential area.

I went back into the house and sat down across from Jewel.

"What was it, dear? My wife wondered, noticing me trying to make sense of what had happened.

"I really don't know. Trance seemed very upset... wanted to talk with me alone. Then before he said a word about what he needed to discuss, he took off in a frenzy."

"Girlfriend problems…most likely. He is a young boy."

"Last I talked to him a couple weeks ago, he wasn't even dating," I recalled. "Honey, this is something more than that. He was scared."

"Why don't you reach out then—call him and offer to go see him."

"I tried to call him back before I came in. He didn't answer."

"I know how much he means to you. Benny, why don't you get in the car and drive over to his place? If you put yourself out like that, I'm sure he'll respond. A man his age can get embarrassed about the strangest things—look at your son," Jewel chuckled, having witnessed Dion's erratic behavior after a disappointment or setback.

"You're right, Jewel, my love. You're always right… Wright's are like that," I quipped, referring to my last name, Wright.

Why I would think Trance would go home, I couldn't have answered other than Jewel had suggested it. Still, I headed off in that direction, a twenty-minute drive. When I neared his place, I knew from experience that the parking was not ideal close to his building. I, therefore, went around the block to where there were no vehicle restrictions.

Bloody Bad Luck...Again

The evening had darkened as if in a hurry to hide a secret. In a moment's time, the cloud cover shielded the moon and heavenly stars. There were no streetlights and the only illumination was from the porch lights in front of the small homes. I parked and was about to get out of the car, when I noticed a man running down the street like a sprinter—I froze in terror.

It wasn't that I recognized the figure. Instead, it was the fact that the imagery was identical to what I had witnessed one other time in my life. Every germ of the emotional pus that I had worked three years to squeeze beneath my conscious awareness, had in the time it takes for a star to flicker charged like an assault soldier to ravage my senses.

Was it bloody bad luck? Was I doomed to live the rest of my life knowing that at any instant the sense of inner peace I had tentatively embraced might be erased?

I watched the dim outline of what I was sure was a male streaking along the sidewalk. Then, the scene continued as if it might have been a recording track stored on the hard drive in my mind. A car screeched around the corner, seeming to be in pursuit of the creature that I now assumed was in mortal danger. As the individual saw the vehicle coming, he broke right, apparently to hide in the bushes...it was too late. Rifle fire opened from the front and rear passenger side of what I now viewed as a van. The figure taking the barrage of bullets froze momentarily before dropping like a tree sawed off at the base.

The probability of the man surviving, I judged to be minimal. His body jerked madly in every which direction as one shot after another pelted his torso, abdomen and limbs: the force of the bullets held his body upright until finally he keeled over. As I was gazing upward in horror through the windshield of my car, I noticed the vehicle from which the gunfire had come disappearing into darkness. Still, I was able to discern that it had no license plates.

As had been the case when years earlier I'd seen a man gunned down, nobody was on the street and not one resident had come out of their home to investigate the origin of the noise. Another similarity was that I instinctively flung open my car door and ran over to see if I could assist the man...that's when I fell over weeping. It was Trance Williams. To me, he was a mere boy. I had adored him and I know he had looked up to me for inspiration—the same Trance that only minutes before had come to me for council. He was oozing blood, red liquid coming from at least eight observable fresh orifices in his flesh.

He was wearing nothing but the same thin t-shirt he had on at my house, making the wound holes and the red staining all the more grotesque. I took off my coat and wrapped it around his chest, trying to keep him warm. Then I pulled out my cell phone and called 911.

Fortunately, I knew the name of the street. In seconds, I had ordered an ambulance—though I could tell it wasn't the type of vehicle that would be needed to transport Trance to his next destination.

When I bent down to try and speak to him and ask him what happened, all he could do was stare back at me with a blank face. I could tell that life was rapidly gushing from his body. I heard the sound of a siren approaching. That's when Trance reached out with his right arm, grabbing my elbow and pulling me toward him.

"Read the papers," he whispered. "You'll know what to do." Then he stopped. I watched as he tried with all his will to take another breath of air. It was a small one. As he exhaled, he attempted to instruct me further. "They're in…"

Trance never finished his next thought. I wish he had. That he wasn't able to, cost me a heap of suffering, and nearly my life.

His head rested on my lap. The bleeding from the neck first pulsed and then slowed to a dribble as his heart quit—I could feel the wet hot liquid as it seeped through the heavy fabric of my black jean pants. I sat numbly on the ground. I waited, knowing exactly what to expect. Soon the detectives would arrive and…

The siren sound was getting louder, alerting me that the authorities were approaching. I then sensed a vehicle come to a halt several feet from where I was sitting.

The lights were flashing white and red. There were voices but I couldn't make out what they were saying. A man exited the vehicle and ran over to me. He flicked out his badge to display his identification, and at the same time perfunctorily introduced himself as Detective Dick Howell of the Detroit Police Department. I could have written his script for him. It was the same one I listened to at the first murder scene.

"You a relative?"

I shook my head.

"I'm sorry you had to witness this…we'll take it from here," he advised me as he lifted me to my feet.

By then the damp air was soaking up the sound of police squad cars descending on the murder scene. Howell asked me a couple of questions. Another officer fresh on the scene called out to Howell who then sternly instructed me to sit, pointing to the sidewalk. When he returned a moment later, for a second time he used both hands to lift me by the arms like a barbell. Then he walked me off a short distance to a dark area in front of a home.

"Did you know this man?" Howell asked.

"No, sir." I lied. "I happened by chance to be out here walking."

The deceit popped out as a visceral knee-jerk response. Only later, would I be able to excuse the wrongful act with the explanation that I needed to distance myself from an event I instinctively knew would suck me back into a traumatic situation.

"What about the driver or anyone in the vehicle? You're sure you couldn't make out details of the car or driver?"

"I'm positive. It was dark. I saw it was a van of some sort but I couldn't tell what make—oh, yeah, it had no plates." I was shivering but not from the air temperature. It felt like a motor racing inside my ribcage causing a quivering sensation all through my body. "Look, I don't know a thing; this is really upsetting."

"Do you have some identification?"

I reached for my wallet and handed Howell my driver's license, watching as he wrote down the information. I could see by then that several citizens were observing the scene from a distance. The ambulance attendants were covering the body.

"What about a phone number?" Howell asked.

"(313) 760-2349," I managed to pass out of my chattering lips.

"Why don't you take off, son?" Howell proposed. "I'll get in touch with you if we need to speak with you again."

It was the strangest impression that came over me as Howell suggested I leave. I had to be mistaken but I'd have sworn he wanted to get rid of me.

I walked up the block to where my car was parked. I sat behind the wheel and wept. It was over an hour before the police, emergency team and crowd left the area. I never moved. I must have been invisible in the blackness of night because nobody paid any further attention to me.

Finally, I started the engine. Then I took off for home.

I'd been traumatized in the past so I understood the symptoms. When Jewel saw me, blood staining my shirt and around my neck, she shrieked. It was a déjà vu experience for her, just as it had been for me.

"Twice?" she shouted in disbelief.

She broke down in tears and we sobbed in each other's arms.

"Trance?" she posed hesitantly.

I nodded, explaining to her the few details I could.

Fortunately, both of my children, Dion and Shana, were out. I showered and went to bed…sleeping was another story. I twisted and turned all night. The few times I must have drifted off, I awakened with a profusion of sweat and the dreadfully real imagery of Trance pulling me toward his butchered body. Then his words: Read the papers. You'll know what to do. They're in…

The words zipped through my mind. I broke them into syllables and watched as they each moved circularly in my head. They seemed to march as if in a parade, each revolution bringing them back for my inspection. I tried to make sense of their meaning. It was an exhausting exercise that ran what I thought was hundreds of full cycles before I'd drift briefly into sleep, only to then be drawn back into the experience.

I rehearsed the evening's events. Trance had been distressed when he came to see me. Then he ran off for some unknown reason. I went to find him. When I arrived close to where he lived, I saw him charging down the street. Then there was the van and rifle shots. Finally, Trance dropped to the ground.

He had to know he was in danger, that somebody considered him a threat. It was definitely not a random, recreational shooting by some demented teenagers. The papers had to be the key. Something Trance knew was so threatening to somebody else that they wanted to kill him to prevent him from speaking. The documents must have contained some sort of proof regarding... perhaps a crime.

It made sense up to that point. But how would I know what to do? To address that question, I'd need to have knowledge of the contents of the material that Trance had mentioned. Yet that was impossible for me to determine unless I knew where the papers were. That was where the fatal rupture occurred. Trance died before he was able to tell me where to find them—round and round I went, always terminating at the same dead end.

There was no reason to mention his final sentences to anyone else. In fact, after several days of deliberating where he might have put them so that I would be able to examine the contents, I gave up. Bloody bad luck for

Trance—damn good luck for whomever he was about to implicate in a serious crime. I concluded that the trail ended with Trance's last breath. Some unknown party had been saved by no more than a single instant in time.

In a way, I was relieved. What would I have done had Trance been able to instruct me regarding finding the answer to this puzzle? If they did incriminate another individual or group, would I have risked my life, possibly the safety and wellness of my family, to step up with the evidence? Especially I wondered what action, if any, I might take given I knew that Trance had been killed over that very information. I was unburdened ethically and morally for the matter could go no further—at least that's what I was blessed to believe for some time until…

Perhaps before going further, I might solve the mystery of how this became the second murder I'd witnessed—it has no direct weight on this tale but does provide an understanding of my background and how I had known Trance. In addition, it might excuse any deficiencies in my ability to scribe this fascinating story for the truth is that rather than an author…I am a manager at an automobile factory in Detroit, Michigan.

Once upon a time, I had been a factory line-worker and during that same era of my life I considered myself an aspiring musical composer, lyricist and performer. The truth is, I was quite talented. In fact, only hours before the tragic murder I observed three years before watching Trance gunned down, I had been in New York, about to sign a real-deal musical contract with a major recording label. Then, at the last instant, the execs decided that my material didn't fit with their lineup of artists and they nixed me out of their world as easily as placing an "X" in a tic-tac-toe game.

It was devastating to me. My family and I had sacrificed for a decade so that I could pursue my career. In my heart I believed I had promised them that success was just around the corner and that when it happened I, Benny Wright, would be providing them a lifestyle greater than what I'd ever be able to accomplish as a mere blue collar worker.

In an attempt to ease the pain I was experiencing, I stopped to have a beer before going home to share the bad news with my beloved wife and children. That was when I saw the stranger shot and killed in a fashion that was nearly identical to Trance's murder. The duel catastrophic events of not being signed to the record deal and then viewing the shooting set in motion a cascading torrent of foolish decisions on my part that nearly cost me my family.

It was during this phase of crisis that by chance I met a man named Simon Ritter. He became a dear and devoted friend—even better, a mentor. He encouraged me to write the story of my life, not as a professional project but as a therapeutic tool. I did. In fact, after completing the manuscript I thought I was doing fairly well. My life settled down and I was able to advance at work.

I had deleted the quest for fame and fortune not with a single keystroke but rather, if I recall correctly, closer to three-hundred thousand key taps, not counting revisions.

That was two years plus a few months before…slam! I was back in trouble. This book is my second experience with journaling as a therapeutic intervention.

CHAPTER 2: THE MOTOR CITY

During the years I yearned for Benny Wright to be a known figure in the entertainment world, the truth was that my name wouldn't have been easily recognized by the mass of mankind on the street. Still, in the local music scene in Detroit, Magic, my stage name, had been known as a quality artist. I had written and produced my own music. My lyrics were all original. As a performer, I was acknowledged as one who could bring excitement to any audience watching me.

It wasn't uncommon that I'd be called on to appear at a street concert or less often as a third act at a larger venue. I also think, if I were to be objective, that I had a reputation for being generous with my talent. It was not infrequent that I would help some of the younger artists with paternal advice on their careers—odd considering that mine never took off.

For Trance Williams, I had a particular fondness. He went by the stage name of Triple-XXX. I'd occasionally volunteer to help him out by playing as a backup musician for one of his performances. My caring was expressed in other ways as well with Trance; there were a few times that I let him perform beats and lyrics I had written.

It may have been that when I looked at Triple-XXX, I unconsciously noticed a similarity to myself. We were both nice looking men—we shared a similarity of skin color, a creamy tan reflecting another piece of background that was common to each of us; our fathers were African-American and our mothers Caucasian. Our height and build were nearly identical, each of us weighing in at just under two hundred pounds.

There was more that bonded us. He was a clean-cut kid who created music that represented a similar offset as mine did to the gangsta' rap that featured filthy language and violent themes—both of us wrote about topics that were clean and wholesome, and our lyrics were nearly void of profanity. Our lines relied more on clever manipulation of words and phrases—the employment of alliteration and assonance, rhythms and cadences—to create a poetic journey.

Well over a decade separated us by age—Triple-XXX was only nineteen when he was gunned down. Sure, he'd get headstrong, but never did he display a cocky attitude; youthful exuberance would best describe his persona. I

20

thought of Trance as a boy-man, maturity in many areas was far beyond his years.

I was also drawn to him because I believed he had a fair chance of rising in his career. If I had to choose from the local up and coming hip-hop artists who would have the greatest chance to make it out of our city and into the national music scene, no doubt it would have been Trance Williams. In fact, his stock value had already begun making a notable jump. He had only months before his death signed a contract with Z & Z Beat Records. He was cutting tracks and entertaining in front of larger performance audiences.

All of these factors contributed toward me not being able to bury the tragedy of my second murder scene. I wanted more than anything to shake off the gory images and sad memories haunting me. I prayed for it to fade from my mind so that I could go on with my life in peace. It was not to be: no matter what I tried, the murder of Triple-XXX preyed on me.

Three years earlier, both before and while encountering my own life crisis, it was a normal part of my routine to stop off at Jimbo's, a tiny spot near my place where I'd horse around with the guys and have a beer. I was not visiting with the same frequency I had in the past, but I'd stop by enough to catch up with my best friend, Craig, and another buddy, Link.

So it was not by chance that the afternoon after I witnessed Trance's murder, I went in for a drink—I shouldn't have. Everyone was gabbing about Triple-XXX. Nobody had a clue what happened but everyone had their own theory that they were certain was correct. Most important for me was that just hearing the matter being tossed around by the customers sickened me, so much so that Craig took notice that I didn't look well.

"Benny, I haven't seen you looking this bad for a few years. I know you cared a lot for the kid."

I didn't say anything but I dropped my head enough for my friend to take it as an invitation to investigate my gloom.

"You know anything about it?" he posed.

"Not really," I lied again.

"I'm sorry, man. They'll find the bastard that did it."

"I hope so," I responded with such dispassion that it contradicted the sadness evident on my face.

"How's Jewel and the kids?" he queried to change the subject.

The beer mug in front of me was full. I nodded to let him know that they were well; then I lifted my drink and in one motion tilted the glass until the bottom shot a reflection of blue light straight up at the ceiling.

"One more should do it, Jimbo," I called out to the proprietor. "I'm walking home and need some love."

At that moment, Link had joined us. "One more is all any of us want," he declared with a pat on my back. Then he took a seat by my side. "How many one mores is the question," he jived, loud enough for most of the patrons to appreciate his attempt at humoring away the guilt suffered by those that made a sport of losing track of how many one mores they'd called out.

"Let me rephrase it for Jimbo then. One last one," I pronounced.

"Have it your way but I'm in the mood to drink to Trance, and it's going to take an ocean of suds for me to get over missing him. You have any idea, Benny, what happened?"

I had no idea why Link would ask a question similar to Craig. Still, I kept quiet, shaking my head to assure him that I was as blind to the details of the kid's death as my friends. Unfortunately, his bringing up the subject again caused me to agitate over the unpleasant thought that I'd now lied about Trance's killing to three people.

I had never been a heavy drinker. Rarely would I have more than one Bud and I'd make it last whatever amount of time I'd be at the bar. Ordering the second had to reflect the fact that fibbing takes a toll on the conscience—greater amounts of deceit require larger doses of vice to palliate the soul. Two barely did it for me that evening.

During the past two years, my career as a factory manager had been on the rise. I was brought up to work hard and never cheat my employer out of a fair day's labor. As a result, I was respected. During my early years on the job, while I considered it a temporary gig until my music took off, upper management would approach me with offers to join their club, initially as a supervisor. Their promise was that I could earn my way up the ladder—I'd always refuse. Then after resolving that music wasn't going to be part of my plan for the future, I buckled down at the factory. No doors had been closed. In no time, I was pushed up the chain. In fact, I'd already attained the title of department head and was receiving hints that I might be next in line for an upcoming divisional position.

Every weekday morning, I'd get up at five-thirty and take off for the plant. The shift began at six-thirty but religiously I'd make it a point to be there at least fifteen minutes early. The morning after going to Jimbo's was no exception. Then the day unfolded uneventfully, except for not being able to put Trance out of my mind. After I left work, I went over to Arnie's Coffee Bean & Tea Leaf, a privately owned shop where I still went frequently to meet with my mentor, Simon.

I can say confidently that he possessed a wisdom I'd never known in another person. He was the furthest from any definition of a formally religious man, yet he had the type of faith and confidence in the human spirit that was deliriously infectious.

He hadn't changed a tad in appearance since I met him three years earlier—I might not have either. Simon buzzed his shiny silver hair in a crew using his own set of shears. I had several years to go before I'd be looking at my next decadal birth celebration—forty—while

I knew my spiritual guide had a couple years before tip-toed like a sleep-walker past sixty.

Fortunate for the little guy, his spine hadn't surrendered even a fraction of an inch of his five-foot-six inch frame...and his dietary habits had kept his figure tight and slim. Most important, I was certain that the man would someday reach his final moment exuding the same signature youthful, childish, attitude that defined his remarkableness. He maintained the softness of gait of an Indian hunter and the stride of a gentleman who had renounced worry. Even his smooth, clear skin remained unblemished.

An avid reader, he was deep in concentration on a book when I came in. There was also a newspaper on the chair next to him. He was sitting by himself and didn't look up, although I could tell he sensed my presence long before I came to his table. He reached to pick up the paper so I could sit directly next to him.

With it in his hand, he flipped over the sheets until he had it open to the front page. Pointing, he directed my attention to another article addressing corruption in the city government.

"This city is a cesspool of fraud, political filth and vice. Now the Director of the Department of Public Works is being prosecuted. His little scheme allowed him to steal millions from contracts for new sanitation trucks," Simon smiled. My friend was an expert on the topic of local governance, particularly the offenses of leadership, and he delighted in sharing news of all their shenanigans. "Believe me, before it's over he'll be suing the city for his pension, compensation benefits and unlawful termination. It's a sick puppy we're living with... and at the national level it gets worse," he chirped.

"Dangerous place," I mindlessly added to the list of Detroit's least attractive titles—though I didn't mention my association with Trance's murder.

> *Is Detroit a dangerous city?" Simon mimicked my statement. "Take a listen to this," he howled as he snatched the paper and then turned to an inside page. "Government officials in Detroit have recently been heard bragging that crime, once believed to be on a pace to supplant auto manufacturing as the most recognized headline of the metropolitan area, has been on the decrease since the 1970's. In fact, the authorities hailed a 2006 study concluding that crime in downtown Detroit was lower than the national, state and metropolitan averages.*

Simon paused to smite the article by smacking it on the edge of the table. "There's more these goons are gloating over, Benny. Pay attention," he playfully instructed as he read portions of the article.

> *A 2007 survey concluded that Detroit had only the sixth highest rate of violent crime among the twenty-five largest cities in the U. S. Better still, an FBI report showed that between 2000*

and 2004 there was a drop of 23% in violent crimes in our city, and the downward trend continued up to the issuance of a study in 2008.

The Detroit Police Department's Crime Analysis Unit is not to be outdone in celebrating their great achievements in law enforcement. They proclaim that by introducing gaming in the city—as well as a neighborhood stimulus plans—crime has decreased 24%.

My friend could have been a great satirist, evidenced by his entertaining presentation of the newspaper article written by a journalist who had to share Simon's disgust for corruption and governmental deceit. "Why would any fool pay millions for a home in Mission Viejo, California—by the way, rated about the safest city in the country—when for a literal tenth of the price you can settle in Detroit? For god sakes, Benny, let's call everybody we know and enlighten them to the best kept secret in America."

Simon wasn't finished. "That material I read you, it was taken from the *New York Times*. Benny, it's one of the few editorial sources left on earth that still occasionally publishes a well-researched article. The writer did his homework before completing the piece. Listen!"

I continued my inquiry into crime in the Windsor-Detroit area, known as home to over five million people. I found conflicting data, Mike Stobbs, the reporter, disclosed. *Frankly, I was*

> *scratching my head trying to figure out what was truth and what was fiction. It seems a private, so-called unbiased group— CQ Press— studied presumably the same FBI statistics and concluded that the Motor City was the most dangerous in the country, nosing out its neighbor, St. Louis.*

> *Their findings did not go over well with officials embarrassed by the report. They were quick to damn the maverick analysts at CQ Press for preparing a paper doing groundless harm to Detroit, as well as other cities they claimed to have been senselessly besmirched.*

> *Evidently when somebody at the FBI was approached for an explanation as to the divergent interpretations, his take was that analyzing the two studies against one another was worse than comparing apples to oranges—instead he proposed the analogy of watermelons to grapes as being a more fitting representation.*

"All fruits to me," Stobbs humored, "but I'm not an FBI man."

The article concluded:

> *Most alarming to me as I studied the matter was a notation in 2008 that the Detroit Police Department under-reported homicides by misclassifying criminal incidents.*

"The Police Chief of Detroit must have kept his mug shut," concluded Simon as he pushed aside the paper. "I can't find anywhere that he issued a rejoinder. The man employed to protect us didn't have to; the protuberance of his nose, I'm sure, would do the talking for him."

We all know statistics can be twisted, shaped and contorted. But what shocked me about Simon having chosen to tee off on this piece that was highlighting confabulated data pertaining to assessing the safety of the center of the auto industry in America, was that Trance Williams had been killed right in front of me within the last forty-eight hours, hardly an indication that we were living in a safe city.

Over the course of the next few days, as Jewel filled me in on the news reports, it became evident that the man (Trance) the media referenced having been shot dead, and in cold blood (that was an indisputable fact) for some unimaginable and unexplained reason, had been determined by the police authorities to have succumbed to a random, drive-by incident. When I heard that, my thoughts immediately returned to my earlier discussion with Simon. Something was not on the up and up for the police to publicly make that statement.

I'm not certain if I said anything to my wife to suggest that The Police Department's conclusion might be inaccurate. Still, for some reason Jewel expressed unmitigated doubt on her own. "A drive by shooting? Is that possible, Benny?" she scowled.

I scanned the newspapers for days after she'd summarized her conclusion. There was no follow up; it was as if the murder never happened. Granted, Trance was not a widely recognized celebrity. Still, he had a large following locally and even regionally. It was news! Yet the police were content—more accurately eager—to dismiss the matter. Could the explanation for their indifference be as benign as a statistical preference? I wondered. Again my mind referred back to the article Simon had shared with the intent of placing local corruption in bold letters.

Trance Williams may not have rated a full battalion of detectives investigating his case. But as it was, only one had been assigned to look into the murder, though even then little time and energy had been deployed toward examining why this innocent kid had been gunned down...gangland style. Unimportant as it might have seemed to the authorities, Trance's killing was about to begin a war. I hoped I could sit on the sidelines and watch. Yeah, right.

Whatever was the motive of our dear police department, within days it became evident that their nonchalance didn't sit well with Trance's family, especially his big brother. There was nearly a decade separating the two men, with four other siblings between the oldest and youngest children of Vernon and Gloria Williams. Marvin, the oldest sibling, was big to the family not only due to being a healthy sized specimen and the most senior of the offspring, but also because he was one of an elite group of athletes in the National Football League.

He was quarterback for the Miami Dolphins. So honored to have him as their on-field leader, the team secured the 28 year-old star two years earlier by coming to terms with him on the largest contract in team history, an eight-year, one-hundred-thirty-nine million guaranteed deal—that's big.

The young man had all the wealth, fame and esteem one could dream of, yet he hardly fit the expected mold of a wild, foolish kid enjoying too much of the good life at too early an age. He refrained from drugs and alcohol. He dated, but was in no hurry to marry. He had sought out advice to help develop a sound investment program…his only extravagance was doting over his family. If he could assist his brothers and sisters developing their talents, he was avid about doing so. Thus it was a fact that from the time young Trance first decided to pursue his career as an entertainer, he had the full backing of his big brother.

Then, after being murdered, the loss had the full outrage of Marvin. That is, when the star athlete contacted the Detroit Police Department and expressed his opinion that his brother might have been targeted for murder, the police sloughed off his concerns. They insisted that they found nothing to suggest wrongdoing. It was their contention that, sadly, Trance had been in the wrong place at the wrong time.

The basis for the family's demand that the police further investigate was that Trance had called home the day he was murdered. He spoke hastily with his father. Later Mr. Williams would describe his son as sounding "terribly frightened" as he said that he might be in danger. His son didn't want to elaborate on the phone but promised he was planning to drive out to the suburb where the family home was that evening so he could discuss his concerns with his father. Piecing the story together, I have to conclude that Trance's plan was to conduct some sort of business with me, and then counsel with his family.

The case had been assigned to Detective Steve Ramon. Marvin and the family had waited at home initially to allow the police time to look into what happened. When they heard the position of the department, they couldn't let it rest. They had already conveyed to Ramon information about the call from Trance to his father. Still, the official police response was that unless the family could produce some evidence of wrongdoing, there was really no basis for allocating precious manpower of The Department to continue investigating beyond what they would routinely do with any other motiveless criminal event—basically cursory police work with the objective to prepare a report.

Ramon insisted that they had done due diligence in terms of scouring the neighbors for clues but they had come up empty. At most, there were a couple residents reporting that they did hear the sound of screeching tires and of rapid rifle fire, but could add no other details.

Trance had no criminal record. Ramon explained to Marvin that he had personally interviewed several of Trance's friends, but even after that the detective had concluded that nothing out of the ordinary had been taking place in his private or professional life to raise suspicion of an intentional killing.

Most remarkable was that the sole witness to the murder, Benny Wright, had never been contacted by the police for a follow up interrogation—it was a fact that only myself and Detective Howell knew. According to the information presented by Ramon, Benny Wright didn't exist—but he sure did to the Williams' family.

The funeral for Trance Williams was held on October 23rd.

Understandably, Marvin was far from satisfied with the police position, as well as the obvious refusal to thoroughly investigate what the family knew was crime. He made numerous attempts shortly after the funeral to dig up additional information that might shed light on the murder of his brother. He had been advised by a city official who refused to go on record, that the Detroit Police Department was sensitive to a growing narcotics business in their city. That situation had led to a series of documented murders. As a consequence, the more incidences that The Department could categorize as killings unrelated to drugs, the better it would be for those rotten statistics that were speaking to a law enforcement system failing to confront a nasty infestation of undesirables.

Trance, however, had never used drugs. His family, as well as those friends that knew him intimately, were certain of it. Sure, he was a rapper, but his image was clean and true to the values of the mom and dad that raised him to follow—he loved to perform and create music, pure and simple. Thus, they wondered, what could the boy's murder have to do with organized crime and narcotics?

Displeased with the potential drug angle, Marvin persisted by using his influence to press buttons at the Detroit Police Department's headquarters, going so far as to be awarded a private hearing with the Chief of Police, a man named Randolph. He walked away with the same   if-there-is-anything-we-come-up-with-we'll-let-you-know story from the top man.

Certain that he was being stonewalled by the police, Marvin over the course of the next several days decided it would be best to spend some of his free millions of dollars looking into the matter independently. His resolve to do so wasn't lessened after I contacted him to disclose that Trance had come to my home late the afternoon of his murder, that he was anxious and agitated, and that he had expressed concern for his safety.

I had known Trance's family quite well for several years. When I first began tutoring him, he was only in his early teens. Then, after I retired from my own career in music, Marvin approached me. He explained that Trance had a connection with me and he asked if I'd be willing to mentor him, especially help shape his voice and his overall brand.

I agreed. The outcome was favorable to the extent that Marvin and the Williams' family held me in high esteem. Thus, after I revealed for the first time that I had witnessed the shooting but never been contacted for a follow up interview by the police, Marvin went ballistic. Again, he requested to see The Chief. After being granted a second meeting, he came away certain that he was dealing with some sort of cover up—Randolph insisted that there was no report of a witness. He even called Detective Howell while Marvin sat in his office, listening as Howell responded dumbfounded at the assertion that a witness had been briefly interrogated at the scene of the murder.

It was after being rebuffed by Randolph that I talked again with Marvin. He explained what happened, advising me not to come forward. It was his thinking that until he had a handle on the reason for the obstruction of the investigation by Detroit P. D., I might become endangered if I formally reported to the police or media information that was contradictory to the official police position.

I did tell him about Trance's last words, trying to convey something to me about papers. Still, I had nothing of substance to report regarding the nature of the documents that Trance was referring to. Marvin made a note of it. He then advised me to keep that point as well to myself until he and I spoke at a later date. That suited me just fine.

*****

Here the story took a very curious twist that I would have never imagined. When I went through my period of despair several years earlier, creating havoc for my wife especially, there was another woman involved, Cookie Acosta. My relationship with her had always been pure business; she sang back up for me on numerous tracks I recorded and would appear with me in live gigs.

In terms of pure beauty, as well as raw sexuality and sensuality, Cookie was unrivaled. She had her baggage due to having been physically and sexually abused during her childhood, but her character had survived unblemished. It may have been that the trauma she endured early on built the foundation for the high ethical principles she strove to live by, as well as the determination and devotion she poured into whatever endeavor she was pursuing.

Her education had been limited by her having to drop out of high school to escape the horrors she faced living with the sadistic behavior of both her father and brother. Yet she later managed to complete her GED. She then started to take college courses—she was innately extremely bright and excelled in her studies once she was out from under the adversity of her birthplace.

A bit more history is necessary to explain how Cookie reentered this episode of my life, and what role she would play in the unraveling of the mystery of what happened to Trance Williams. Once the entire drama of my escapades three years earlier played out, and I had written a book about it, Simon had the bright idea of turning it into a musical. In fact, I participated in developing the book and songs for the piece. When I presented it to Simon, he was intrigued. He, in turn, showed it to a friend of his that ran a small non-equity theater in town. The director of the theater thought that the musical was worthy of a live production. He also came up with the idea of each role being filled by the real character. Thus, all of the principles became stage actors.

We had a blast. Jewel, my children, my ex-agent Garland, his secretary and best friend of Jewel, Georgia, my friends, Craig and Link, the owner of the saloon I visited from time to time, Jimbo, Cookie Acosta, and a few of the regulars from his bar, all shared in the experience. In fact, we were so enthused we decided to stick together as an amateur troop. We were able to put on a couple more shows during the ensuing months before…whatever happens that naturally brings non-remunerative activities to a halt.

Later, after our group disbanded, and because she wanted to continue on stage as a hobby, Cookie went on to play the role of a criminal investigator in a play entitled, Courtside. The production died a quick death, but the budding actress found her groove. That is, her act as a sleuth hit a cord for the lady because after the lights burning out on the play, Cookie was writing a new story into her life. It was to be Cookie Acosta with the title, Private Investigator, after her name.

All along, she had been amassing college credits with no specific matriculation in mind. Thus, when she began bundling the courses she had taken and then outlined with a counselor what she'd need for a degree in criminology, she realized she wasn't that far from a real goal—it seems that her lust over the music industry tanked concomitant to me putting the same dream to bed.

It was only months before the murder of Trance, that Cookie completed her degree. She had earned the right to call herself a full-fledged private eye. While in school, she had struck up a tight relationship with one of her professors. This man had the rare power of vision to see that hidden inside perhaps one of the most alluring female anatomies on earth, was a talented and dedicated young woman who might serve a vital need in his business.

John O'Keefe was not only a full professor in criminology but he also headed his own small but esteemed private investigative service. There was one problem. O'Keefe had a remarkable fondness for alcohol. During the past of couple years, he recognized that his dedication to his business interests was waning and his reliability lessening. He realized that if he didn't do something about the situation, he'd lose his prestige, and then his clientele.

The real issue, however, was that what most would have assumed to have been the "problem" for O'Keefe, alcoholism, was not. In his opinion, alcohol was a substance that offered a sure fix for any and all of life's petty and not-so-petty disappointments and trials; his favorite brews were miracles of nature that made daily life a dream. Understandably, abstaining from alcohol would have been to his detriment. His concern was how to enjoy his substance of choice without guilt or shame, without the onus of having destroyed his career by neglect.

What this man needed was Cookie Acosta, a young lady who could service his clientele with a smile or a smirk, a snicker or a sneer, an enchanting and entrancing young woman that would make all the suspicious wives, cunning husbands, greedy businessmen or nasty politicians forget that John O'Keefe even existed. It was not his intent to abandon his following, only to graciously evaporate into the suffusing fragrance of Cookie Acosta.

Ah, but to drink without having to take responsibility for the untoward consequence in terms of business deterioration. What a vision, and it could come true if only... So he offered the fledgling investigator the opportunity of a lifetime. She could come to work in his office and learn from an experienced pro the ins and outs of the business, eventually having the whole filthy firm to herself. Cookie needed about one second to deliberate. In no time, she was working cases as if she'd been in practice for a decade.

She also had a history with Marvin Williams and the Williams family, one that I had orchestrated. Not long after I had backed out of the absurd caper I'd pulled with my family, and about the time I began working with Trance, I suggested to Marvin that in addition to myself, Cookie might be helpful to my young protégé. Cookie had one of the best ears for sound I'd ever known. She also implicitly understood style. She was a whiz at identifying what might be the up and coming rhythms and beats that could possibly spark the career of a new artist.

Marvin was agreeable to employing her to help with Trance…until he saw her. I should have advised her to tone down her appearance the day they met because the second Marvin set eyes on Cookie, little brother's career had been demoted. It took eight months of on and off dating before the relationship petered out. It was one of those situations where both parties realized it could never work and mutually agreed to terminate on good terms—a rare animal in the dating world.

It wasn't until the flames of romance were extinguished that she was introduced to Trance. When she finished putting her final touches on the boy, his act was as smooth as a hustler's handshake. Marvin vowed he was indebted to her and proposed ways to satisfy what he thought was an obligation. Cookie had refused money or any form of compensation for her services to Trance. By the time Trance was murdered, Marvin had never been permitted a way to repay her.

Cookie attended the funeral. She wept with the family. Then later, when Marvin shared with her the disreputability of The Department, she begged him to let her snoop around and see if she could catch a clue or two about why the police were acting dishonorably. Marvin was hesitant. He knew that, at some point, the assignment might become dangerous. He knew that Cookie was not a seasoned professional, increasing the odds that she might get herself into trouble. When he used these arguments to justify his decision to refuse her offer, she persisted, going so far as to remind him that he had wanted to reward her for having helped Trance—this would be the only payback she would accept.

Finally, he gave in. There was, however, one other hurdle she'd have to jump before officially taking over the investigation. Her boss, O'Keefe, had expressly informed her that the one type of case he didn't take was murder investigations. Fraud, infidelity, corruption, drug abuse, heisting gems, stashing money from a spouse; these were the bread and butter items on his profit menu.

He might get a percentage for locating a precious

stone or have a bonus thrown in by a mother with two children if he identified where her husband was squir- reling away millions in cash. Murder cases were typical- ly straight hourly fee deals, plus they entailed a greater amount of risk than they were worth.

Cookie knew the rules. She also understood that O'Keefe was deteriorating. In her opinion, the man was lonely and fear-ridden in spite of his professed wish to die by the juices of Johnny, Jim and Jack. (He loved whisky and had no preference as long as the brand start- ed with the letter, "J," Johnny Walker, Jim Beam and Jack Daniels.) She went out to lunch with her boss to argue for her to take on the Trance Williams case. She de- scribed it as an extraordinary opportunity that involved a close friend, something she felt she owed the family. In the end, her boss refused to give her permission. Cookie went home, not defeated but instead knowing that the battle was just beginning.

In an attempt to focus the attention of peers, instruc- tors and clients on her intellectual merits, at school or when going to work, she purposely avoided enhancing her beauty and sexuality. This time it would be differ- ent—O'Keefe had no idea what was coming.

When his assistant came back to the office in a pair of designer jeans and a translucent rust-toned top reveal- ing she'd dispensed with the bra, he relented within a second—Cookie had a way of getting what she wanted. O'Keefe must have left the office for one hell of a party with the "J" boys, because he wasn't seen again for two days.

It was November 3rd when Cookie officially assumed the lead in her maiden murder investigation. Her first assignment was to set up a meeting at the Detroit Police Department—specifically, the officials responsible for the decision not to handle the Trance Williams case.

She met with Ramon, still the officer officially assigned to Trance's case. It was a short visit—Cookie was out of the office within fifteen minutes. The discussion with the Detective proved as she expected, pointless. She'd later explain to Marvin: "He wasn't lying. I will tell you he has to be one of their youngest and most inexperienced officers…plus he comes off as one of the laziest human beings I've ever met," she huffed.

"They put a flunky on it!" Marvin decried. "It had to be intentional so they could stall the investigation," he reasoned.

Cookie would later explain her bosses take. "O'Keefe told me he's seen it over and over that captains or other superiors put rookie staff on a case as a strategy. If for one reason or another they want to make it appear that the matter is getting attention when in truth they have no interest in it, or were being ordered by superiors from above to let it die, that's how they do it."

Cookie left the meeting with Marvin carrying a list of friends and associates of Trance's. She reasoned that Ramon likely asked a few redundant questions as part of his "investigation" and then took off. Therefore, she decided to double check with the people Trance knew best. She also told Marvin she'd be spending time at the library reading recent editions of The Detroit Free Press and Detroit News newspapers. It was a tactic she'd used in school when dealing with mock investigations. "You'd be surprised how many leads you can get canvassing the papers for local news stories about political debates, economic conflicts and community relations," she informed Marvin before departing.

In addition to the associates of Trance's that she planned on contacting, she had other names she wanted to approach. Cookie was going to handle her breakout murder investigation with absolute professionalism. It meant that nobody with any information relevant to the crime would escape interrogation or be shown mercy if they failed to fully cooperate.

Marvin hadn't informed Cookie regarding what I had experienced with Trance on the evening of his murder—my interview could wait. But Garland was a top candidate to provide valuable information. He was Trance's manager and agent; even more, he had risen to become a very powerful figure in the music world.

His presence was felt far beyond Detroit. He had influence throughout the entire Mid-west region of the country, and he was even reported to have sufficient strength nationally in the industry that he could command a piece of the action when regional stars were shipped off to larger agencies on one of the coasts. If you were going to be anything in the music field, you had better hook up with Garland. He could make and break careers with a smile, the same one.

Garland had been a friend of mine since grade school. In fact, he, Jewel, and I spent the years of our early schooling together—I say "friends," though it would be obvious to any human being on the face of God's earth that Garland was a man lacking in sincerity. Truth be told, he was a wily, cunning and greedy man in business while an equally shallow, disingenuous and frivolous one in relationships—he'd proudly admit to his shortcomings, and with no less enthusiasm proclaim his will to never change. Jewel and I kept him in our life much like a bad habit.

Cookie knew Garland well. She tolerated him but never trusted him. There's little doubt that one of the reasons her career as a vocal artist never took off was due to the fact that she intentionally selected a lesser-known agent, and refused to reward Garland with samples of her passion. Garland professed that one of his most cherished activities was building careers, but his favorite was destroying them. I know that since grade school Garland wished to conquer my wife, his jealously over my having won her heart must have tipped the scale in the direction of him undermining my career—Cookie and I both owed a large part of our failing to Garland.

Still, he was around, always lurking in the background,

trying to convince me I was his "best buddy." Even so, I knew he was waiting for a tragedy to befall me, so he could have another play at my wife.

When Cookie called his office, she reached his secretary, Georgia. She was informed that she had just missed the man. Georgia offered to leave a message for Garland to get in touch with her—that was the first attempt by Cookie to contact him.

Failing to receive a reply after leaving a second similar request, Cookie wasn't going to give up. "My Lord, girl that man holes up in his office for hours. I can't get him to answer me sometimes." Georgia's southern lips twanged the nasal sound of the cold that had been tormenting her for the past week. "I can give him a message but I have less influence on him than all those husbands of mine I've buried," she cackled.

"That sounds like a story," Cookie laughed.

"I'll let you in on a little secret, darlin'. They were all sentenced to die when I married them."

"You're serious?"

"That was the past. I've turned a new leaf. Got me a free man now, but if he keeps up his nasty ways I'm going to send him to meet the others."

"Georgia, you sound like a remarkable woman," Cookie commented with an unmistakable tone of bewilderment.

"Remarkable, no. I'm just lonely," Georgia admitted cheerlessly.

"Welcome to the club."

"What an honor, huh? Well, listen, dear, I'll leave number three for him…can't promise a thing."

What was keeping the exec so busy he hadn't returned her call after she left her third message with Georgia?

The answer to that question is one of the rare truths I'd ever discover about Garland, and actually where the next chapter of this story begins.

CHAPTER 3: SLAM DUNK SLAMMED

Addictions! Forget the never-ending debate regarding the cause being a genetic/physiologic factor or environmental/stress-related. Whatever might be the explanation behind these dastardly habits, they are pervasive. I'm not a scholar but Dr. Harvey Plum is; in fact, he's a professor of abnormal psychology at Michigan State University—he's a humorist as well. I was acquainted with him through a close friend, and at dinner one evening at that buddy's home, Plum was present: since the topic had weaved its way into my thoughts, I brought it up with him. As soon as I did, his face lit up joyously. He then volunteered a lengthy lecture on the subject.

"I'm convinced that every human on earth has at least one, if not two or more," he asserted confidently.

"Sounds absurd? Start counting. There are millions and millions fitting into a huge number of categories of these unhealthful indulgences. Did you know that today it's estimated that one in eight Americans struggles with some form of alcohol or drug addiction—that's not even including the unimaginable number legally addicted to substances kindly dispensed by a range of medical practitioners from generalists to internists to psychiatrists to pain management specialists?"

"I never thought of it like that, my wife, intrigued by the subject, replied.

"What other behavioral patterns can become addictions?" he continued our tutorial. "Tobacco, gambling, shopping, eating, watching television shows and sport events, listening to music, engaging in sex, lying, playing sports, exercising, working and even being on the internet can turn into biggies. I suppose there are smaller numbers of people helpless to extricate themselves from a host of other less notable habits. Anything can be an addiction—we're told—if the behavior is something we can't stop doing in spite of the consequences being self-destructive."

"I guess that would include nearly everybody, unless, of course they're perfect like me," I joked.

The professor refused to let me slide. "We already know your addiction, my friend."

"Really? You don't even know me," I laughed off what I wondered might be arrogance. "If it's so obvious, why

49

don't you tell me?" I challenged; admittedly, I felt a bit defensive.

"Satisfying the members of your family."

"Wonderful guess. Somebody tipped you," I chucked, now less alarmed that he was about to zing me with some dark compulsion even I didn't know I suffered. "Yes, I agree. But you might not be aware that I'm cured of that one," I quipped.

"You're never cured from a bad habit. The best you can do is fight for your life. That's why there are so many groups supporting every imaginable destructive behavior pattern known to man—and their members join for life. Relapses are as predictable as maggots."

"What's your addiction? Isn't that a fair question since you already publicly exposed mine?" I couldn't help trying to even the score.

"You...and your fellow man."

"All of us?"

"Yes. To keep humanity from forgetting the boundless power of love," he smiled. "Now, may I continue my lecture?"

He was right. I'd learned from Simon, and from my own near-tragic life experience, that love is the only ingredient necessary to keep us healthy. I nodded for him to proceed.

"What happens if we tally up the victims of each category of addiction? We're talking about hundreds of millions of sufferers. Take sex as an example. It's amazing but think about all the patterns in this classification alone—there's compulsive masturbation, need for extra-marital affairs, multiple sexual partners or one-night stands, consistent use of pornography, unsafe sex, phone or computer sex—now actually titled cybersex—prostitution, exhibitionism, obsessive dating through personal ads, voyeurism, sexual harassment, child sex and incest, and molestation and rape.

"Get it? The conclusion is indisputable; addictions are an epidemic," he cheered. "Chances are everyone has one creeping somewhere. We may not see it on the surface of our acquaintances and relatives because for most people their choice of deviation acts the part of subterranean termites, invisible unless you crawl under the house, at which point the invader might be eating away at the foundation. The truth is that these insidiously destructive patterns can hit a tipping point in the time it takes for a dying light bulb to flicker; then they can turn potentially deadly due to one additional turn of the screw."

"That's why I brought up the subject," I informed him with a hint of sarcasm. "There's a fellow I know," referring to Garland, "that shockingly had a mean one."

So it happened that this mournful commentary on the ravaging impact addictions might have on the human condition brought the conversation back to the swaggering and self-endearing character of what I'll label a supporting actor in this drama, Garland.

To the untrained mind, the man would be qualified as a poster boy for all that is glorious in life, a symbol calling for celebration. He's The Man, the one individual everybody would love to swap places with. He's relaxed, confident, trim and healthy, energetic and . . . happy. If he had, for example, an addiction, I never suspected it, and I never heard one rumored by anyone I knew.

But the truth was that Garland was one of those closet compulsives. His defect belied the fact that beneath the surface, he was a fairly typical guy. In fact, as I'll point out presently, he suffered from what would likely be the national average of addictions, what the psych guru professed from his calculations to be approximately two mal-adaptations per person—and Garland's were like fraternal twins: The first was making money. The second...losing money. To his misfortune, these can both be whoppers.

One of the wonders of the Internet is that people are permitted near complete secrecy while engaging in dirty little idiosyncrasies. For Garland, the habit that leveled him to the same plane as his fellow humans was that he loved to gamble. What placed him still on a different elevation from most common addicts was that he had huge amounts of free cash flow—Garland was single, never been married, and had no children. For a man still in his mid-thirties, he was so rich and rolling in green that he might have planted a lawn of hundred dollar bills, and then watched it grow more wealth.

What in the name of roasted marshmallows, graham crackers and melted chocolate could induce this specimen to engage in acts of self-destruction? I'm not sure there will ever be an absolute answer to the question. I knew that he was a shoe-in to be inducted into the Greatest Bull-Shitters of All-Time Hall of Fame…but a gambler?

I reflected from time-to-time on the matter after Dr. Plum's initial lecture on addictions. Then, later I called him and offered a sketch of Garland's personality and history; finally, out of curiosity, I asked directly for an explanation of Garland's obsession. His reply made sense, though it was a stretch intellectually for me to follow him.

"To be such an ingenuous and insincere creature has an insidiously isolating effect on a person. In the end, the loneliness and disenfranchisement from the mass of humanity smacks back in the form of a wicked gut wrenching sensation," he explained confidently. "In order to not face a reality that would be ego-destructive—the self-recognition of absolute superficiality—a man like Garland seeks unconsciously to punish himself through a ruinous pursuit, one appearing benignly entertaining on the surface but in truth selected for its inescapable pernicious outcome."

It sounded on target to me. Had he disclosed these words to Garland, a mouth full of oversized bright white teeth would have flashed a few inches from the doctor's face. Then after neutralizing the expert therapist with his winning smile, he'd have walked away without ever giving the words another thought.

Regarding his little secret, Garland never mentioned to a soul that he'd sit on the computer for hours a day placing bets on various sports. Making the situation more intriguing, he never invested time in an accounting of his performance. Had he done so, he'd have calculated a most stunning record of poor wagering resulting in a mountain of mounting losses.

Ignoring the absolute figure of debt resulting from his consistent bad luck was dumb enough. But Garland took his negligence beyond that. He never factored in that the online site he was using—one that had kindly extended him credit at a fixed rate of interest, a rate defined as usury—had far-reaching powerful arms. In fact, the extremities had dagger-like fingers trained to squeeze heartlessly if necessary to collect a debt.

Garland must have believed that he had unlimited resources, and his gracious gambling partner site intentionally reinforced the delusion that he was privileged to enjoy a perpetual carnival of pleasure. In fact, during a period of time while Trance Williams was still breathing—a time frame granting my young friend nearly a year more of precious life—Garland's power of magical thinking had graduated to a divinely inspired level. So certain that he had found a method to break the house, he placed a massive wager on a sure thing, slam-dunk spread on several football games. He believed that his strategy was guaranteed to win back prior losses he had accumulated, plus a substantial killing in his favor—he was slammed with the largest beating he'd ever taken. He shrugged it off, vowing that the next time luck would bless him.

So Garland went on his merry—very merry—way. But then one afternoon in May of the year before the murder of Trance Williams, two men came to visit the music honcho at his office. They had not been calendared for a meeting. They never called ahead as Cookie had done; they weren't the type that believed in being rebuffed. When they arrived, they announced that they wanted to talk with Garland. They didn't wait for his secretary to check with her boss. Instead, they walked past the reception area. Then, uninvited, they moved into the inner sanctum of one of music's biggest big shots.

One of the men was built like a whisky barrel. His skin was pitch black in color and the whites of his eyes had a pinkish tone on the periphery yielding the frightful impression they were about to pop out of his face. He stood close to Garland's desk, a few feet in front of his partner, but he never said a word. The other man was much taller and had a frail figure. He looked like a match stick out walking a pit bull, an animal the lanky man knew he could unleash with a mere loosening of the rein.

The skinny one glanced behind him before swinging

the door closed. "You need to take responsibility for your account."

"I'm good as gold. You didn't need to come out of your way," Garland jubilantly informed them.

"It's four hundred ten thousand, plus expenses. Now you have until tomorrow afternoon to settle your account—"

"Not so fast. Let's talk this over," Garland proposed with a clap of his hands. "I have a couple deals closing—"

"We'll be staying overnight at the MGM Grand," the speaker announced, in no way impressed by Garland's dental endowment.

"Brother," Garland stammered an appeal to the broad muscled man, "help me out here."

"We'll be billing all expenses to your account," the taller man declared. "Now at four tomorrow, we'll be meeting you here. Don't make us wait."

"Where am I going to get that kind of money so fast?" Garland posed with a wincing movement.

"Four o'clock!"

The talker signaled to his enforcer that it was time to leave. The muted man then stared assuredly at Garland, the flexed musculature of his face and neck along with the austerity of his expression driving home the point that it would be an unpleasant meeting if he failed to satisfy their demand.

Sitting alone at his desk, Garland would have been seen sweating, something he rarely had occasion to do.

After a half an hour, he took hold of his cell phone. He then placed a fateful and fatal call.

"Hey, hey, Garland here," he sung out in the friendliest of voices. "Been thinking over that proposal you mentioned the other day. Why don't we get together and hash out some of the details—I'll give it a second go-over? How's that, my friend?"

That evening Garland received a call from a man named Javier Mejia—unknown to Garland the two men who had earlier in the day come to his office were employed by Mejia. He also could have had no way of knowing that Mr. Mejia's bosses owned the debt to the gambling site used by Garland.

After speaking kindly to Mejia, he would be given relief for the four hundred ten thousand, plus expenses. How wonderful compared to the options offered by the two enforcers representing the gambling entity holding his debt—pay up or be busted up, or possibly killed. But with Mr. Mejia's deal (again, to avoid confusion, unbeknownst to him, Mejia and the online entity were one and the same), Garland had a third alternative.

It was a deal made in heaven. All Garland had to do was pay up by collateralizing the professional careers of clients. Big deal. Everybody was about to get rich—and Garland was going to become even more powerful than he'd ever been. Luck. Some people get it all.

CHAPTER 4: ROUGH DIAMOND DEAL

The calling of Garland's debt and the murder of Trance Williams—occurrences separated by only eight months—were two events that were circuitously but definitively connected. Cookie would eventually be tracing a path backward in space and time, from Trance's murder to Garland's meeting with Mr. Mejia. Had she the opportunity to examine the papers Trance had mentioned to me on the evening he was gunned down, it would have made her job a lot easier. She would have additionally discovered that some months earlier, Trance had traveled the same road she was about to explore. If her destiny proved to be similar to the rising star, then she would also end up dead.

The Midwest region had never been a stranger to the hip-hop music world. In fact, much of the innovation in the field came from imaginative types that first established themselves in Chicago, St. Louis, Cleveland, Kansas City and Detroit: Eminem might be the most recognized Detroit product.

What seemed to stimulate the creative spirit was a wide-open atmosphere. This was in contrast to the consistency of sounds being produced on the coasts or in the South. This was because in the Midwest, there were no rules or established patterns. The style of the rappers in each of the main cities was different from one another. Even within a particular city, the participants in what were called rap battles might be presenting entirely different approaches and styles to their art.

What this meant was that talent would be spawned in the Midwestern states but later sign lucrative recording and entertainment contracts with large money operations on the coasts. There were people who recognized this talent-draining trend. They wanted to capitalize not only on the earning potential of these home grown artists but a lot more. Two of the key players in this big money battle were brothers, Raphael and Enrique Parra, both men with little interest in music and less in regional community pride.

These ruthless men were not Americans but rather Mexican citizens. Their purpose in controlling the local hip-hop industry was to own a laundry factory, human machines bred to clean dirty money: the brothers operated the largest drug cartel in Mexico.

One of their top officers had come up with the idea of investing in musical talent as opposed to many other more transparent ventures used to turn illegal dollars into legitimate currency. These men had truckloads of cash rolling around cities with no place to deposit their fortunes. If they couldn't convert it to spendable money, it was nearly worthless. Thus, they had millions of dollars to throw at their newly spawned ingenious enterprise.

Mr. Mejia was a front man for the Parra brothers. In the preparation of the business plan, he had scoured the records for the online gambling service owned by his bosses. His intent was to see if by chance, there might be a heavy hitter like Garland who if given free reign might get themselves into a difficult spot. Thus, it was by plan, that not infrequently Garland would have his ego puffed up by being sent notices informing him that his credit limit was being increased.

Mejia couldn't have called it better. Garland took the bait, digging himself into a pit from which there was no escape. Recognizing that the subject was trapped, a week before Garland was informed that he had run out of credit for his gambling habit, Mr. Mejia had personally attempted approaching him via phone to solicit his participation in a program aimed at driving a key stake in the cartel's venture.

When Mejia first contacted Garland, his mission was to bring Garland on board. Then, once under the grasp of the Parra brothers, the agent would be expected to gradually place the rappers in his stable under contract with the new firm the Parra Brothers were setting up. It was further assumed that the artists themselves would encourage selected associates to join Garland and then become clients of the new entity. Garland listened to the stranger who, in vague terms, outlined the business proposal. Then, he refused meeting with the man to discuss it further.

There was no offense as far as Mejia was concerned. His policy was to always offer a man a choice. Therefore, when he sent his two hatchet men to talk with Garland it was to let him know that he could cooperate or not, but either way there would be consequences.

It wasn't that bad for Garland. After all, Mejia was not asking for miracles. He was only expected to start off by bringing aboard his new acts, plus as contracts came due for the established people he represented, he was being politely requested to bring them into the "family" as well.

Since he'd permitted himself to be ignorant of the debt he was building, Garland also chose not to focus on the fact that he was now complicit with some nasty hombres, people who could at any time they chose tighten the noose around his neck. What mattered to Garland was that he had magically dissolved hundreds of thousands of dollars of debt. Then as a bonus, he was set to share in a cut of each of the new lucrative contracts that would be signed—more wealth and more power is all that he sought from the onset.

Garland began by introducing a number of his clients to the wonderful opportunity of making money for doing nothing other than moving it in circles. It was easier money than recording tracks or going on tour. A number of months into the new business, he proposed the program to a recently signed client, Rough Diamond. Named for the clarity of his sound, the golden-amber color of his skin, the buff of his physique and the rawness of his undeveloped presence on stage, he was assessed as an up-and-comer. He was a young man that many thought had a crack at making a name for himself as a top hip-hop artist.

The real appeal of Rough Diamond was his teen-like appearance. In truth, he was twenty years old. His fast-paced and power driven beats with gangster themes struck a note with the teen and pre-teen market. Enhancing his attractiveness was the fact that he was a superb dancer and had written a song entitled, Lay Down, Kick Out. It was seen as being on its way to popularizing a new dance craze.

Garland's attempt to bring in Rough Diamond was at the behest of Mr. Mejia. Garland would periodically receive calls from Mejia instructing him about deals that needed to be arranged with Garland's clients. Peddling the program to the various artists was the responsibility of Garland but Mejia outlined—actually dictated—the precise terms for each contract. The conditions were so enticing that Garland generally had no problem enforcing the mandates ordered by Mejia—as he'd joke to his new lord: "I've never even had to twist an arm." But that was before Rough Diamond came along.

The young man was under contract with Garland for two years. During that span of time, Garland might act to greatly support his career or destroy it. Mejia was adamant that if Rough Diamond (or any of the artists being offered the opportunity) protested, he or she should be informed in no uncertain terms that their refusal to cooperate would result in a most unfavorable consequence to their future as an artist.

On the surface, the deal being offered to him was amazing. The artist was to sign an exclusive entertainment contract with a company controlled by the Parras, LimeyShadeBlood Enterprises. The terms were extraordinary for a still unproven rapper. Rough Diamond would receive fifteen million dollars, all of which would go into a company owned by the young man. However, he was to then deposit in equal installments nine million of the amount over the next year into another business called Detroit Production Services, also owned by the Parras. They were giving dirty money with the left hand and taking part of it back sanitized with the right. They believed that their share of the proceeds from their actual investments in the artist would pay additional clean money returns: the pattern was being replicated with a full lineup of top rappers.

It was a deal that couldn't be refused by a ghetto youth who might otherwise end up, if he were lucky, with a factory job working hourly shifts for the rest of his life. Sure, based on his own virtues, Rough Diamond might continue as a second tier act in the music world. He might even rise higher than that. But to amass six million dollars, an amount he was now guaranteed up front, was unimaginable. He knew it. Garland knew it. The Parra brothers knew it.

The kid Rough Diamond wasn't dumb—he had little formal education but his instincts were sharp. He asked Garland for an explanation of why the generous offer was being made. He also insisted that he be provided with an outline of the risks to him for moving such large sums of money from one account to another.

Garland assured him that in the business world, the amounts would attract no attention. He added that for his client, the only danger was that his career could stall, which he assured Rough Diamond was exactly what would happen, if he refused. In other words, should he not assess the matter reasonably, he'd be locked out of the industry.

In the end, Rough Diamonds' response might prove that, in fact, he wasn't too bright. He called Garland a "cheap thug" and assured him he was not only going to contact an attorney, but he also planned to break the contract he had with Garland and report the attempted coercion to the police. After informing Garland of his plan, he then walked out, furiously slamming the door.

That night, June 18th, he called his pal, another young hip-hopper named Triple-XXX—it was Trance Williams who had introduced Rough Diamond to Garland. The two were very close and when they met up later that same evening, he revealed in detail what had happened in Garland's office.

Two days later—June 20th, Rough Diamond, born Brent Calhoun, was found dead in his apartment. The police determined the cause of death to be an amphetamine drug overdose—the only problem being that Brent Calhoun had never used drugs in his entire life. He had sermonized to Trance Williams on many occasions his view that substances were a conspiracy to keep poor people disempowered. Both rappers shared a determination to stay clean regardless of the perverse forces and influences surrounding them in the record industry.

There were obvious questions pertaining to the death of Rough Diamond that needed to be answered. Yet as would be the case after Trance was murdered, the police were content to dismiss the possibility of foul play. The family of Rough Diamond were very poor and had no money for private investigators, although they were certain that the worst vice their son had was a wicked habit of over one pack a day of Marlboro "death sticks."

They didn't know it, but their son's good friend, Trance Williams, had decided to kick the dirt until he created a cloud of dust. Within that murky space he operated as a sleuth. In that capacity, he'd unravel the details of the mystery of his friend's murder, and then some. The fledgling private dick unfortunately made one mistake, a biggie that would lead to him being the victim of murder. At the culmination of his investigation, he showed his hand, emerging out from the soot with an oversized sign painted in red capital letters on his head reading, KILL ME.

Everything he had collected on the subject of Rough Diamond's murder he'd entrusted to me minutes before his death—he fell seconds short of making me aware of the location of the document.

CHAPTER 5: IN A TRANCE

After Rough Diamond was found dead, Trance Williams was stunned. It wasn't only the pain of losing a trusted companion that troubled Trance. It also baffled him that the police showed no inclination to investigate beyond what on the surface was an obvious determination that his death was drug-induced. Trance knew it couldn't be true that Brent Calhoun had done something stupid by getting mixed up with drug trafficking or that he'd violate his firm conviction to abstain from ingesting illegal substances.

He even went to the authorities and met with one of the detectives assigned to the case. The response was no different than what his older brother would confront after he himself would be killed. He kept asking himself not only why the police were disinterested in the tragic loss, but also who would have been motivated to stage a scene making it appear that his friend had been using drugs.

It gnawed on him day and night. Trance Williams, similar to his older football superstar brother, was not a man to let things pass when he was confronted with a glaring untruth, especially when the life of a friend was at stake. Even as a kid, Trance couldn't tolerate dishonesty or injustice. He was a flyweight boy who rather than win a battle by trying to whip an adversary, would study the problem until he came up with a smarter means to defeat an enemy.

His greatest asset was a gentle charisma. Not only were peers drawn to him as a friend, they also listened to him. He would be heard chattering on one subject or another, surrounded by a clutch of other young people. It was this skill that he exploited in the performance of his music, finding it natural to sweep an audience into the mood or theme of his creation. It was that same talent that he drew upon when beginning his examination into the death of Rough Diamond—sadly he proved to be less successful as an investigator than an artist.

Before taking any definitive steps to look into his friend's death, he jotted down, and then ruminated on, the few facts Brent had mentioned to him the evening they spent together just before he was murdered. He used a pink highlighter to underscore the key words he'd written. Then he analyzed them daily.

He knew that in the big scheme of the music biz,

Brent was still nobody. That being the case, regardless of Rough Diamond's potential, why would any record label be tossing millions of dollars at him? His friend had told him it happened, so he knew it had to true. Thus, he was convinced early on that it was a dirty story needing to be aired. His interest was of course, Rough Diamond. But then as he deliberated the staggering amount of money involved, he realized that the matter might stretch far beyond Brent: if there was an attempt to engage Rough Diamond in some sort of illicit deal, might not other young talent ultimately be warped by the same influence?

His first thought was to go directly to Garland and confront him with the information Rough Diamond had shared. But when he considered that option, he concluded that he'd never get the truth. Trance was managed by Garland—as was Rough Diamond—but he'd long before sized him up as a devious and deceitful man who he had to use to his advantage while at the same time keep a close eye on. No, Trance decided to proceed in a different direction.

The career of Triple-XXX had begun in Detroit. My early intervention had helped him improve his presence locally but then by the time Cookie had added her touch, his talent was gaining recognition in clubs all through the Midwest. He had a vast network of colleagues he kept in communication with regularly. Strutting that easy-going, laid-back personality, it seemed that most of his fellow artists took as kindly to him as had his buddies since grade school.

Triple-XXX didn't have the full ghetto background many of his contemporaries did, nor was his music hostile and violent. To the contrary, his appeal was that the sounds he produced were a mild, smooth, oily rap. He relied on music and lyrics that bounced gently rather than as was more common for his fellow artists in the field, sounds that smacked, whacked, banged and boomed for the audience.

Based on Rough Diamond's disclosure of millions of dollars being thrown his way, Trance was aware that the journey of exploring why Brent was murdered—an assumption he considered fact—and by whom, might pose risks. He was wise enough to proceed cautiously. Thus, he decided that in his initial conversations with people pertaining to Brent's murder he'd be cryptic, preferring to use insinuations or innuendoes rather than direct questions and references.

He recalled from his love of reading crime novels that smart detectives kept meticulous notes. Thus, on his computer he created a file with a running diary containing every conversation he had pertaining to Brent, even at times recording verbatim dialogue.

These copious comments, observations and facts comprised the content of the pages he might have believed he'd entrusted to me in some surreptitious location; they were also the same materials that was found on his computer by the party that stole it from his apartment, as well as what he had intended to show to his family when he was to arrive at his parent's home that evening.

The final entry in his journal dated October 22nd, reflected the circumstances that alerted him he might be in danger. It read as follows: *Received a call at three this afternoon. It was from Garland. He didn't sound his normal jovial self. He told me he had warned me to stop asking around about Rough Diamond and said I had become a nuisance to people who don't like to be pestered. He wants us to meet as soon as possible—suggests this evening at the Pico Pong Lounge.*

He added his own reflection on the call from Garland: *He was warning me. I get the feeling I'm next in line after Brent to be killed—I'll be better off than Brent because I know it is coming and I can understand why. I had to do what I did but I might have put myself in a dangerous position by doing so.*

This entry was after Trance had already dug his own grave. It was months before that when he had begun his investigation.

Trance had friends outside the music industry, people he could trust and who had no interest in his business. One was a high school chum who had become a tech guru. Never having attended school for formal training, Cal "Happy" Robinson was reputed to be able to hack his way into any computer system. Whether or not it was true, he kept to himself. He had never had run-ins with the law and promoted a straight lifestyle—a full-time job working for Aaron's Research, a boutique operation specializing in analyzing statistical data based on internet advertising.

"This is fuckin' bad Trance," Happy exhorted after Trance shared information about the killing of Brent. "I suggest you leave it alone—no sense you taking a cap (slang for bullet) on behalf of a guy who is already dead."

"I wish it were that simple, but I appreciate the concern."

"It's more than concern. This is big money. Big money means big players and big players means people who make the rules up themselves, and usually as they go along. You don't know their game," the known-to-always-be-smiling-and-jolly friend gritted his teeth. "Hell, you don't even know what Brent might have done."

"That I will guarantee you, he did nothing."

"No, he threatened. You told me that yourself," Happy reminded him.

"Cal, he was being strong-armed to do something that scared him."

"However you want to look at it. I see organized crime here and you'll be kind enough to leave me out of it."

"I will. I promise."

It was a pledge that Trance broke.

Now more convinced than ever that Brent had fallen

into the hands of criminals, his curiosity to at least get answers overpowered reason. His friend was correct to admonish him about risking everything—career and possibly his life—to go after a truth that that might have been of no value to anyone except Brent's immediate family.

When I had the opportunity to later examine the writing of Trance Williams, I noticed that at several junctures he alluded to what had compelled him to keep up his undying quest into the matter of Brent's death. At first he wrote that he simply wanted to know what really happened. Then his motive graduated. He felt an obligation to intercede in a way that would protect other artists from being exposed to threats and intimidation, and then end up unbeknownst to them partnering in criminal activities.

Then as the commentary continued, as he delved deeper into his research, a new force weighing heavily on his conscience was introduced. Trance sought justice, insisted that the earth be purged of whatever sludge was oozing out of the mouth of evil. So intense was his conviction, that it was almost as if he were possessed by a religious zeal, or he'd had a mystical experience—we might say, quite aptly, he was "en—tranced."

After his talk with Happy, being warned that the likelihood of heavy hitters having killed his friend was high, he deliberated on the point. He thought it made sense, but as far as he was concerned, it was simply a possibility; he wanted an outsider's perspective.

Some months earlier, Trance had met a man named Lance Merchant at a party. Mr. Merchant was an investor. He had backed a couple artists in the past and was always looking to put a few loose bucks at play betting on a young kid he thought might have potential. In fact, he was impressed with Trance and had made an offer but before the deal was sealed, Marvin Williams put up the needed cash so that Trance could avoid having to sell of piece of his future.

Nevertheless, Trance recalled hearing how Mr. Merchant was respected for his business skills, which spread far beyond his occasional hobby wagering on entertainers. He decided to contact the man and ask for an objective opinion. Trance left notes on the meeting.

"I'm not going to mention names, Mr. Merchant. Is it all right if we talk in…like general terms?"

"Sure. Go ahead, young man."

Trance explained what had transpired up to that point in this hypothetical case study, never mentioning Rough Diamond or Garland by name.

"Son, I know what you're referring to. There are people out there that play hardball. Just keep yourself clean, that's all I can tell you."

"But that's what Brent…he was trying to keep himself out of trouble and they still killed him. What's the difference?" Trance said despairingly. Then he paused

74

to consider what Merchant was saying. "You know who it is?"

"We'll never know all the details. Trance, sometimes it is better not to," Merchant cautioned. "You have a promising career in front of you. Hell, I would still like a piece of the action. But if you don't leave this alone, you could lose it all. Do you get what I'm saying?"

The man punctuated his point, two times. Trance Williams refused to heed the advice of the elder, wiser man. It wouldn't be until hours before he was killed, while he was entering most of the final comments in his journal, that he would again reference the meeting with Merchant.

I don't know what got into me. I'm in deep shit—I should have listened to Mr. Merchant.

Trance left Merchant's office with absolute conviction that demonic forces were out there and that he was appointed to stop them. He went to his home and began crafting a strategy to delve deeper, to find out who had in fact killed Brent…and why.

He began by calling some of the rappers he knew in other cities, and a few locals. In Chicago, there was a hip-hopper named FlipSide and another named Beat Up And Down. He questioned each in general dialogue on his cell phone regarding how they were doing with their careers. Then he followed with guy chat about lady friends, sport figures and sport cars. Both conversations were amicable up to that point. Then when he approached the subject of Rough Diamond, the tone changed, but differently for each of the men.

"Dude must have been doing elbows (pound of illegal drug). Got to take it smooth," FlipSide stated without compassion. "Don't' drop Rough Diamond on me again or I'm a busta cap in yo ass (shoot a gun at someone)."

Trance concluded that FlipSide bought the drug overdose sham and otherwise knew nothing—beyond that he plainly didn't want to be bothered. Beat Up And Down was a different story.

"Don't yank his ride (steal Rough Diamond's drama)," he angrily shot out at Trance.

"I was talking 'bout it, that's all."

"Sometimes you do what you gotta do." Beat Up And Down slowly rolled out his statement word by word. "Man don't always ask if you want it."

"I don't understand," Trance responded, clearly trying to lead the rapper toward further disclosure. "Brent killed himself, right?"

"Ah, shit. Kill himself?" the man spoke reflectively. "We all gonna kill ourselves or get killed we don't… play…the…game."

It was an eerie statement, one that Trance logged in his journal. To him Beat Up And Down was all but telling him that he was being dictated to by somebody and might have had a similar ultimatum offered to him, deciding wisely to take the bucks and "play…the…game."

The responses varied as he contacted colleagues in

Cincinnati, Kansas City, Milwaukee, Omaha and St. Louis. His overall impression was that most of the singers had no idea what happened to Brent and couldn't have cared less. There were, however, a couple of the men he talked with who seemed to speak in circles. Trance interpreted their cumulative responses to suggest that there was theme in their riddling conveyances. That is, the industry was being criminalized and there were many artists who had come under the authority of evil—yet none were willing to speak openly on the subject.

Most convincing was a rapper he had performed with on several occasions in Detroit, CountMeIn. His real name was Wayne Basie and he was rumored to be the grandchild of the great Count Basie. Trance concluded that Wayne had inherited gifts from grandpa and was by far the best of all the regional performers, the one he was sure was headed skyward.

When he called Wayne, he was greeted kindly. Trance suggested they get together and Basie eagerly agreed. They met at Jacoby's German Biergarten, a pub with a small performance area where new talent could first take to the stage. Trance thought of this particular spot because, by coincidence, it was where both Basie and he had their first experiences as public figures.

The establishment was located in an historic neighborhood of Detroit called Bricktown. In fact, it was only a short distance from the Courthouse. Trance was a

fiend for old movies and particularly for some odd reason discovered W. C. Fields and Mae West. Each time
he walked past this spot, he chuckled at the thought that
long before he was born the great comic actress, Mae
West, had come to court to face a charge of public inde-
cency—he loved thinking she was as much a riot in real
life as she projected on screen.

Wayne, his body covered with tattoos meandering
from his shaved head down the neck and then roaming
all the way along both arms, was already at a table with
a beer in his hand. When he saw Trance, several years
younger than him, he sharply nodded his head as a wel-
coming gesture, but displayed no facial movement.

Trance was wearing a pair of Levi jeans that looked
like they had decided to quit. They were relatively new
in that they retained both the thickness of the fabric and
the deep blue shade. However, the waistline had slid so
far down Trance's skinny buttocks that they no longer
served to cover his ass, instead the task was consigned
equally to a pair of underwear that handled the lower
portion of the anatomy and a long plain white t-shirt
taking top-side duty—the miracle was that while he
strode down the street, up and down the sidewalks, and
into the establishment, the denim material halted short
of falling to the ground: it was as if an inner glue or series of bobby pins kept them in place.

Trance's wardrobe was never going to land him in the
poorhouse. He wore the same style attire as if it were a

uniform, both on stage and off. The only article of jewelry he adorned was a small diamond stud in the right ear lobe. This contrasted notably with Basie who featured poundage of gold in the form of necklaces, bracelets and rings as well as two large diamond studs in both ears and a heavy silver chain-banded watch freely dangling off the left wrist. I wondered each time I'd bumped into the artist, if he were truly in the Count Basie lineage how the clean appearing granddaddy might have judged his progeny.

They spoke for a while about the music scene, sharing a pitcher of tap beer and an order of nachos with melted jalapeno jack cheese. The conversation went well until Trance mentioned the passing of Brent Calhoun.

"Bitchass mothafucka. That boi knew nothin' 'bout ice (crystallized methamphetamine) or yayo (cocaine). Hell," he chuckled, "he didn't even do weed—he was whita than you."

"You don't think he killed himself?" Trance innocently asked.

"Don't you be bustin' me, bringin' the popo (police) down on me."

"Police? Payce (peace), cuz. Just want to hear what you're thinking."

Wayne leaned close to Trance so as to not be overheard. "These aren't common wiggers (white males acting like thugs) playing hustla'. These are bad ass gangstas and they're not niggaz or whitie…got it? It's all about Benjamins ($100 bills)."

"I'm tripped out here," Trance responded, intentionally trying to convey that he was dazed and confused by Basie's assessment of the situation.

The call by Trance for further explanation, however, must have alarmed Basie, cautioning him he was dangerously running at the mouth. "I'm outtah here."

Trance would later record that he knew Basie was scared, exactly the state he would have been in had he used the same power of reason possessed by the bejeweled artist. Instead, he felt a stronger call to action.

Basie was represented by Garland. Could there be a connection? Was he beginning to see dots, even recognizing there could be lines drawn from one to another, and that collectively they might form a figure enlightening him as to the befuddling mystery? He conceived that soon he himself might be another spot in the drawing.

It was about then that a recollection came to him, something important that he had failed to log after Rough Diamond's death. When he met with Brent just before he was killed, the name LimeyShadeBlood Enterprises was mentioned. Rough Diamond had explained to Trance that after he would have received the bulk payment of fifteen million, the monthly installments were to go into that account.

After LimeyShadeBlood Enterprises popped into his mind, he stopped to look up the name on the internet—there were no references. The inexperienced investigator lacked the sophistication to know what other means were available to identify and research a business entity.

Still, reasoning that the word "enterprise" had to mean that some form of commerce was being conducted, he decided to pursue the matter further. Here is where he violated his buddy, Happy Robinson. If there was anyone who could flesh out a piece of information, it was his tech genius friend.

There was no infraction to his promise in asking Happy to identify if such a company existed, and if so where it was located, what was the nature of its operation, and who were the principles associated with it—the broken trust by Trent would come later. In the meantime, Happy was "happy" to assist. In less than a day, he had an answer for Trance.

LimeyShadeBlood Enterprises was incorporated in Delaware but registered in Michigan. Its legal address was a post office box in Detroit and the officer of record was a Javier Mejia. The registration indicated that the corporation had been established to engage in musical production and distribution.

Trance had never heard of Mr. Mejia. He knew it would have been foolhardy to try and communicate in writing by sending a letter of request to the post office box. Further, he reasoned that if Brent Calhoun had been told he was to make deposits to that corporation, they must be associated with a bank where they had some sort of business checking account.

That's where the breach with Happy came in. If his friend could be convinced to help him to find out where the business did its banking, then he'd be able to gain invaluable information. Trance would write in his journal that Happy was not "happy" about participating in the caper, but finally did consent with a promise that his name would never be associated with the highly criminal act of hacking into an institution's computer system in order to attain information on one of their customers.

This broken promise to Happy was not to be the last on Trance's part. Trance never imagined that his notes would come to any purpose other than for him to have a daily accounting of his activities. If the outcome were to be what he sought, exposing the corruption in the music business, then he would hand over the factual material but his personal documentation would never be known to anyone but him.

"If the account is held in one of the larger institutions like Citicorp or Bank of America, I might come up short of accessing the financial details," Happy forewarned Trance before he engaged in the project. "I'll have a better chance if it proves to be at one of the smaller banks."

It turned out that the account was at Dearborn-Detroit Federal Savings Bank in Detroit. Robinson was able to gain access to statements of transactions. Furthermore, he discovered that the account for LimeyShadeBlood was opened in the names of Raphael and Enrique Parra, both using the same post office box for communication.

Trance picked up copies of the financial dealing of the company from Happy's apartment. He then went home to examine the material that included details as to checks deposited, wire transfers into and out of the account, and source names of those who had participated in the monetary exchanges. As he began outlining what he was previewing in the material, he noticed first that the account had been created only eight months earlier.

Few transactions at first—the number increases month by month, Trance jotted in his notes. *Several essential facts re: the bank ledger for LimeyShadeBlood. Unbelievable. One: It's like a parking lot—money comes in and later leaves. Once the deposits are made, identical withdrawals follow—one transaction washes out another. Two: The amounts are large, hundreds of thousands at first—then increasing to millions.*

Three: It's amazing. Names with deposits—artists I know from around the Midwest region—I've worked with many—most are clients of Garland. Four: Damn. Money from LimeyShadeBlood Enterprise account deposited into three separate accounts—all handled at Dearborn bank.

Trance's final note indicated he was planning on hitting up Happy one more time.

During that visit, he twisted his friend's arm to take another step. This time he needed him to access the same information on the three accounts where the money was being shuffled after it left LimeyShadeBlood.

It turned out that the Parra Brothers controlled each of the three accounts. The money deposited in each of them was being used to fund various purchases and investments ranging from homes in Malibu, California to condominiums in New York City to real estate development projects mostly in Southern California and Chicago. He also saw large sums being dispensed to individuals, none of the names recognizable to him.

As he reflected on the material he had illegally attained, he expressed his distress regarding the list of depositors in the LimeyShadeBlood account.

My God! I call these people "bro" and I respect many of them. Can I blame them for falling into a scheme that was making them rich? But at least one of them has to have a conscience, feel some guilt and remorse. I need just a single soul to join forces with me.

There were names he already had cause to suspect, including CountMeIn and Beat Up And Down. But as he continued scanning the names, he was most shocked over one in particular, Blue Angel.

I can't believe it. He's the coolest of all the rappers I know. Blue Angel—he's a top-of-the-world guy. He's potentially bigger than CountMeIn. He's the next Eminem; we all see it coming. Trance's enthusiasm as well as disappointment jumped out of the words.

Yet Blue Angel was taking down millions of dirty

money—top on the list—returning fortunes of cleansed green bills for the Parra Brothers, men about which Trance still knew nothing.

It wasn't only Blue Angel, however, that caught his attention. Names like LucoBratzi, My Fairy Lady, Bumpkin and Bottom Phish were among the group of entries. Noticing these people on the list irked Trance, for he knew them to be at the lower level on the success chain, yet they were handling million dollar transactions; most of these people were giving almost all of it back to the Parra Brothers.

I'm going to look into the Parra Brothers now. I have no idea who they are. That was the final entry of that session.

Two days later, he had his answer, one he easily attained, without even asking another favor of Happy Robinson. All he needed to do was Google the names. Within minutes, he understood what CountMeIn was trying to tell him with his words: "These aren't no common wiggers playing hustla'" or "…they're not niggaz or whitie."

These were top-notch drug leaders from south of the border—not the one separating Michigan from Indiana and Ohio. The Parra Brothers were fearsome men running the largest drug cartel in Mexico. Trance understood by this time that these men had billions of cash that they couldn't use legally until it had been purified.

They were making massive investments in artists for that sole purpose.

What he never addressed in his notes, and may not have considered, was that people like Garland were now being doubly, triply empowered in the industry. Garland could singlehandedly alter the lineup of entertainers for whatever reason he chose; artists like my friends, Link and Craig, and myself for that matter, were being denied success based on decisions having nothing to do with talent.

Trance did wonder why he was exempted. On the one hand, he felt blessed by the omission. At the same time, however, it concerned him. He wondered if it had to do with his brother. Garland let it be known that Triple-XXX had funds of his own and might not only refuse the invitation but make trouble if he was slated to fall under the evil thumbs of The Parra Brothers. Then he also calculated that when his contract with Garland came up for renewal in a few months, he might be fingered like the rest of the victims.

Fingered? Sounds so benign.

CHAPTER 6: ONLY THE GOOD DIE YOUNG

Even after assembling the lethal evidence Trance now had at his disposal, he kept the findings to himself. He might have been contemplating what if anything he was going to do, because for a period of almost two months—between early July and the beginning of September—he made no entries in his journal. It was almost as if he'd forgotten Brent Calhoun's murder, or wisely decided to leave it rest. More likely, however, was that this timeframe coincided with an intensely creative period during which he was preparing material for an upcoming series of live performances.

He left on a regional tour and was working out of town for five weeks. This was on the heels of the two-month void of commentary in his journal, bringing the total period he seemed to have dismissed the matter of

Brent Calhoun's murder to over three months—up to the first week in October.

When he returned from the road trip, he spent a few days relaxing with family and friends. It was after that when he once more addressed the murder, making it clear that far from considering dropping the matter, he had achieved a greater level of resolution that he was going to set the industry once more on a legitimate path.

It was also during this phase of his life, when he free-associated in his writing about his views on hip-hop and the importance of "the movement": *God's bright light of benevolence burning in the heart of man compels the rap artist to enlighten his audience to His truth.* He defined as his personal goal to assign every beat and lyric he created to a ministry dedicated to what appeared to be a divinely inspired spiritual purpose.

Trance then made another statement. He wasn't about to give up on Blue Angel. He had faith that once he talked to him in order to explain what he had uncovered regarding the drug money coming into the coffers of so many local artists, that the star would open up by admitting his own misguided participation, and then join forces with Trance to bring down the corrupt influence now poisoning their beloved field.

Naively, he believed this man could be trusted more than any of the other artists. Also, without having ever discussed it directly with him, he believed that he and Blue Angel shared a vision for hip-hop in that both of their styles were similar. Blue Angel, like Triple-XXX, also had an educated mind capable of approaching his career intelligently.

Blue Angel had been on tour himself and was due back in town days after the above notation was made. Trance announced in that entry on October 13th that he was going to contact Blue Angel as soon as he returned and then had a few days to rest. Thus Trance Williams waited. It took longer than Trance anticipated to set a time to see Angel, but the next entry—October 21st— described the meeting that took place that evening.

Blue Angel had invited Trance to be his guest for dinner at Bourbon Steak in downtown Detroit. They both arrived near nine o'clock. At first they talked about how their respective tours went. Then Trance approached the topic he came to address. He began by mentioning that he was aware there was some matters taking place in the industry that were making him uneasy and he thought Blue Angel might be feeling the same.

The host listened to his guest as he explained that he was sure Rough Diamond had been killed for threatening retaliation toward Garland. Then he shared how he had subsequently discovered the investments being made by the Parra Brothers. He also disclosed that he knew it was drug money that was being laundered by these criminals who were coercing talent to take deals that were outrageous and destructive.

He went so far as to level with Blue Angel that he

was aware Angel himself was participating, but Trance softened the blow by telling him the reason he wanted to talk to him was that he knew Blue Angel had been forced under threat to fall in line. Now with the information he had, together they could bring to an end what was only going to become a worsening crisis. Holding nothing back, he further mentioned that Garland had to be the central figure orchestrating talent being brought into the operation. Finally, he shared that with his contract coming up for renewal in a few months, he might be next to be approached by Garland.

Blue Angel let him talk, not saying a word until Trance finished. He first corrected him by clarifying that Garland hadn't been his agent. Instead, he professed to be represented by Len Wilcox. Trance knew what he was being told was likely a lie in that Blue Angel and Wilcox were known to have had a contentious relationship. In fact, rumors had spread that Blue Angel had some time in the past switched agencies as part of a swap deal between Garland and Wilcox.

The likely fib was hardly relevant once Blue Angel leveled the boom. He delivered to Trance a most unexpected reply. He told him he thought the young artist was grossly mistaken in his assessment of the situation. He insisted that he had never entered into any such monetary arrangement with any party. Without seeming to be defensive in the least, he casually explained that his career was, and always had been, on the up and up.

Then he finished with a stern admonition, one that from the reading of Trance's notes sounded closer to an upbraiding.

"Trance, you're a sweet man and you have a great future. You are mistaken in your accusations. But even being incorrect, you could find yourself in danger by throwing around names of powerful people in a disparaging manner. I'm going to do you a favor and forget this conversation ever took place."

Trance was heartbroken that he would be lied to by someone he looked up to as a model of honor and integrity in the industry. He was also infuriated that Blue Angel had no interest in helping him clean the crud out of Detroit's innovative and unique artistic community.

"I gave you a chance to come clean. I swear I'll expose you with the rest of the actors in this cheap play," Trance threatened. "I'm sick to say it but…you're a coward."

Trance had always been able to straight-talk with Blue Angel, without a lot of hip-hop jargon. But he left with an angry statement. "I gotta jet."

According to his notes, Trance went directly to his apartment. He began organizing the material he planned to turn over to the local police and the FBI. He knew once they had the evidence, the proverbial shit would hit the fan. Nevertheless, in the end, everybody inside and out of the industry would be all the better for it.

The next morning—October 22nd, Trance received an early awakening, a call from Garland.

"Hay, hay. How's my main man?"

"I'm your main man, Garland? That's the first I heard of it."

"You're right...there on my list," Garland crooned. Trance could hear Garland snap his fingers, one of the signature gestures he unwittingly used when verbally fornicating a client or friend. "You think I've forgotten you for some of the good action? Is that what's kicking at your bones? It's coming. Be patient."

"I don't want your action, Garland. I want the corruption to stop and that's exactly what I'm going to try to do."

"This is not a good conversation for the phone. I suggest you be careful with terms like corruption," Garland warned with an uncommonly severe tone. "Why don't we meet, real calm like. I think there's a big role for you. Triple-XXX has just what every dime (attractive woman) is looking for. Heck, you're the up and coming, coming up sky high. Can't you see the future?" Garland sung at him, now resuming is customary jolly spirit.

"There may not be a future. That's what's bothering me."

"Trance, let me tell you something. There are people in the world with unlimited resources and more power than you can imagine. They don't need the protection of police departments...they own them. Don't be stupid.

I'm trying to help you. Your contract is coming due with me, so we'll be talking big numbers very soon."

The rash expression of truth in the words that followed may have sealed Trance's fate, erased a chance for him to live out the natural course of his life. "They're responsible for my friend being killed. They have to be accountable," he shouted as he slammed down the phone.

It was after the conversation with Garland that Trance knew he needed protection. If anyone could help it would be his big brother. He made calls to his family and then promised he was coming home that evening for advice.

By that time, Trance Williams had gone into high alert—it was still October 22nd. It was too late to call a truce.

Trance parked his car several blocks away from his apartment. Then he carefully made his way back to his place, certain that he hadn't been followed. The rest of the afternoon, he spent organizing his notes and making final entries on the computer. He printed a copy of the document, folded it, and put it in his pants pocket. When it was dark, he snuck out of his building through a side exit. He walked nearly a mile in the direction where he'd parked his car.

After his talk with Trance, the agent tried to reach Mejia to inform him of the potential danger. Fortunate for Trance, Mejia was out on business and Garland wasn't able to reach him—it wasn't until later that afternoon when he'd get in touch with him. That permitted Trance to get to his car and then to my home safely. However, by the time he tried to get back to his place, a decision had been made to terminate Trance—immediately.

Guards had been stationed at every possible entrance to his building. Attempting to sneak back to his unit, one of the men commissioned to eliminate him caught sight of Trance. He fired a shot that missed. Realizing what had happened in the short amount of time since he'd left in his car to see me, he took off running in the opposite direction.

The man who followed his first shot with a series of errant bullets notified three men patrolling the area in a van, advising them of Trance's location. Seconds later, Trance Williams would be murdered—the only known proof of his findings were now in an undisclosed location and on a file on his computer. His last breaths of life would be an attempt to instruct me to take action on a set of papers I couldn't have known I possessed.

The killers of Trance Williams had entered his dwelling and then stolen his computer and printer…before he even stopped breathing. Investigating Detective Howell, shortly after the murdered man's body was taken to the morgue, would disclose to an associate of Mr. Mejia that the victim at the time of death had nothing in his pockets other than a set of keys and his wallet, the latter with a few bills, credit card and incidentals—there was nothing of value found on Trance's person; nothing either after a thorough inspection of his car and his apartment, other than the computer hardware stolen. It must have been assumed after Trance's discussion with Garland that he had documented whatever he knew, but Howell assured Mejia that no such evidence was uncovered.

Later, when it was determined to be fact that a printed document of some sort had been produced, the question was raised as to where the copy had found a home. That mystery would burrow in and suck on the Parra Brothers like a tic—they were willing to expend any amount of money and manpower to find and destroy it.

Benny Wright had it.

When Raphael and Enrique Parra came to suspect that, their problems, and mine, were only beginning.

CHAPTER 7: WATCH OUT BAD GUYS

Cookie's early stop at the headquarters of the Detroit Police Department was unremarkable, as was the library research. She decided to make a slight change in strategy, determining that her next step would be to take a look at Trance's home.

He lived in an apartment in the posh Fort Shelby Towers—for a young kid he was already doing quite well for himself even without a "deal" sponsored by the Parra Brothers. He chose the building because the owners had proudly distinguished their unit types with names like Basie, Armstrong, Goodman and Hampton, paying tribute to artists Trance held in highest esteem. In fact, he decided on an upper story Gillespie apartment, affording himself a view of the Detroit River.

He loved looking out at night on the James Scott

Memorial, a giant fountain that when illuminated in orange, yellow and blue tones reminded him of the pyramids. He also appreciated the quiet of the small island sitting in the center of the river where the structure rested. Often during the day, he'd sit and watch the spurting, gurgling and shooting of water. He'd laugh thinking about the story behind the noted public monument. It's what inspired his imagination when creating lyrics.

James Scott, in whose honor the monument was constructed, was a notorious jester, usually veering his humor toward the devilish side. More memorable about his reputation, however, was that he was a gambler, a rare one as evidenced by the fact that he was able to die loaded with green. Reviled by many of Detroit's elite at the time, they graciously accepted his willed desire to leave the city an amount evidently in dispute but between two hundred thousand and half a million dollars, a tidy sum in the year of his passing, 1910.

He did place one provision on the use of the money. The city had to build a fountain, paying homage to the one and only James Scott himself. The prankster wanted the last laugh...and bought it. He also may have been one of the early pioneers in establishing legal mechanisms for controlling funds from the grave, a compulsion detested to this day by the heirs of many rich people.

Each time Cookie tried to gain entry to Trance's apartment she was rebuffed by the police. If Detective

Ramon and the rest of the team thought they would easily discourage the lady, sending her packing back to O'Keefe's office to get soused with her boss, they had the wrong party. Their refusal to open the dwelling to her inspection plainly peeved her.

With the approval of Marvin Williams, she contacted Norman Springer. Mr. Springer was a local attorney who she selected after being advised by Mr. O'Keefe. He informed Cookie that Springer had tried an abuse case against two of Chief Randolph's pet enforcers, and won. The Chief made no secret of the fact that he despised the attorney. Still, Springer had friends he could call on that had influence with Randolph.

Within two days, she had access to Trance's unit. She intentionally took Marvin and one of the sisters, Wanda, with her. Cookie had already interviewed each of the family members to get as many clues as possible about Trance's character and personality. Still, if there was something out of the ordinary about the dwelling—up to that time, none of the immediate family had been granted access—one of his clan might notice it.

Cookie immediately recognized that the family agreed about Trance's most outstanding traits, neatness and order. Even after the police had swept through, the floors were immaculate, the dark hardwood in the kitchen area shining bright as the afternoon sun beamed off the thick lacquered finish. The cream-colored carpets in the living space showing no signs of footprints.

"Cookie, you only knew Trance as an entertainer, sort of the surface of the man," Marvin commented, noticing the investigators gaze as she inspected the pristine quarters. "If you really got to know him, you'd have found him to be the kind of guy who joked that if he had to walk on any surface but concrete, count him out. He hated earthly soil, too…dirty to him," he shrugged with a smirk.

Trance had early on acquired a fondness for modern. The rooms were tastefully but sparsely decorated in a minimalist fashion. As Cookie wandered through the space, the siblings of Trance Williams followed as if expecting to be struck by a ghost. Cookie recognized that they were finding it difficult reliving memories of their dead brother. Still, she poked questions and expressed impressions for the purpose of keeping their mind's alert to the purpose of the visit, to identify anything that might shed light on what happened to their brother.

When they entered a small room that Trance had used as an office, all three stared. In direct contrast to the rest of the apartment, it was a mess. It was not dirt or neglect that stood out. Rather, it was carelessness. Piles of papers, writing tablets and composition books were scattered haplessly.

"Something is wrong," Wanda softly muttered as she looked at Marvin, her nonplussed extended stare speaking to the fact that a neat freak like Trance would have never tolerated the dishevelment they noticed.

The giant man shook his head as he inspected the room. "That's not Trance. He always talked about the creation of music and lyrics in terms of mathematics. That's how he kept a balance between the invention of his work and the discipline necessary to accomplish it. Chaos? He could have never lived with it."

"The police couldn't have done this," Cookie commented dubiously, "could they?" Then she paused long enough to organize her thoughts. "Funny they made no mention of this room looking distinctly different from every other in their cursory report. Hell, they didn't say much of anything in their review of the case. Even a novice would have highlighted this obvious inconsistency."

"Something else, Cookie," Wanda mentioned. "I don't see his computer or his printer. We never received it and we were told it wasn't in his car. I assumed it would be here."

"Did he have a backup someplace?" Cookie queried.

"I'm sure he did. His music was his life and every file he had was on the computer—he had to have duplicates and probably an extra copy on his email or backed up elsewhere," Wanda assumed.

"No sign of it here, is there?" Cookie mused. "Somebody was looking for something…they beat us to it." She stood silent in thought for a couple minutes before speaking again. "Let's take a look at his clothes and inside the drawers and cupboards."

As they entered the bedroom, it was like transitioning

to an altered dimension from the clutter they had just witnessed. Again order was restored. The clothing was limited to a few items; not only did Trance wear the same uniform daily, but he kept only a few copies of each article. In the closet, he had neatly hung a few pairs of jeans. Surprisingly, there were two pairs of slacks, neither of which looked to have ever been worn.

Cookie instructed both brother and sister to go through the drawers and to inspect the pockets of the shirts and pants in the closet. The task produced only a laundry ticket.

"My brother would have never used a washing machine," Wanda proclaimed while holding up the presumed worthless ticket. "Everything went to the cleaners. It's probably a bunch of underwear, socks and pants."

"We'll pick it up anyway," Cookie answered. "My boss says that ninety-nine percent of what you find during an investigation is a waste of time. It's the other one percent that breaks the case. Off to the laundry."

Cookie was a wonder, a work-in-progress—it might be stated accurately that the case was growing her.

No doubt the disturbed and traumatic youth she experienced weighed heavily on her emotions. The damage suffered due to early abuse had especially undermined her ability—better stated, her inability—to sustain intimate bonds. It was difficult for her to trust. She had shared with me that she felt anxious the closer she became with a man. I also can state that to the best of my knowledge, she had few friends, and none with which she shared true intimacy.

Then, after she retreated from music and instead began her study to become an investigator, a transformation began taking place. People dealing with her noticed her changing. Outwardly, there was a sense of lightness she'd never witnessed in the past, as if some of the weight she'd been hauling with her had lifted. She now displayed a doggedness and intensity regarding her career, a determination she had never exerted toward promoting her talents as a singer. That fact, even more than Garland forsaking her, might answer why she hadn't gone further as an artist in that she was a dynamite stand-up vocalist.

As the coming out of Cookie Acosta continued, several traits new to her palate emerged—she was fearless. Based on her distressed past, it would be easy to assume that she'd be weak and easily intimidated by men…and she was, though she had always masked it with a superficial flirtatiousness. Now, however, she was the intrepid cat, undaunted by threats or bullying.

Another critical element of Cookie's transformation apparent to anyone interacting with her during the investigation was a newborn personal habit pertaining to food and exercise. Previously her attention to diet and care of her body had been terrible—neglectful was a better choice of words. Then, out of nowhere, Cookie seemed obsessed with healthy eating, insisting on organic products that was almost exclusively vegan.

But the real show was what she started to do with her physical appearance. From day to day, she'd literally overhaul how she looked. This was especially evident when it came to her hairstyle and head coverings.

"I must say that my favorite hat was a red straw specimen with small turtle figures of varying colors serving as a headband," Marvin laughed as he visualized her one afternoon when they'd met to discuss her progress in the case. "The piece had a grossly oversized brim that gave the effect of her head seeking subterfuge—the investigator hiding from the investigator." He slapped his hand on his knee, unable to contain his laughter.

Wanda also reported to me that she came to enjoy the times she spent with Cookie, also a witness to the peculiar process of watching an adult go through what might have been an adolescent period of identity experimentation. She recalled one morning when Cookie came to speak with her about Trance.

"Her hair was straight. She was gabbing about hot irons and presses she used to get rid of her natural waves. She also had used a stylist that employed chemicals to accomplish the same goal of removing curls. Then not more than a couple days later…there was Cookie," Wanda howled, "with her locks swirling. I listened as my dear Cookie discussed how her stylist volunteered to perm in curls of just the right size. That girl was going to a masquerade party every day."

Wanda again stopped to giggle away the images of the unusual investigator, a woman I knew for certain had long hair that naturally twisted and twirled, though I'd witnessed the same trick of her shearing her head. "Cookie's a gas, no doubt about that being a fact. I couldn't compute why anyone would take out what was naturally there…then pay to put back what was free in the first place.

"Then one afternoon Cookie put an end to the debate about how to tame the beast of a fickle head of hair," Wanda continued. "She had a new beautician. She raved about the kid who had done her hair. I didn't say a word but Cookie's gorgeous strands had been cut to somewhere in the one inch range. Then to top it off, she'd changed the color so that in bright light she looked like a shorthaired apricot." Wanda couldn't control her humor.

"Most amazing was that in spite of all these ego-altering excursions," Wanda concluded after she'd finally calmed down, "nobody would dispute that Cookie appeared equally fantastic in each of her facades."

Thankfully for the Williams family none of this head tripping diminished her effectiveness in becoming a crack investigator.

After finding the laundry ticket at Trance's home, Cookie, Wanda and Marvin drove only a few blocks to Fluffy's Cleaners. Wanda went in to get the last of Trance's clothing items. She came out with a single black shirt covered in plastic. Inside the car she pulled off the protective wrap and as soon as she reached inside the breast pocket she felt a piece of paper. It was a single sheet, folded neatly. The yellow color had lightened slightly due to having been processed during the dry cleaning. It was heavily creased owing to having been pressed.

When she opened it there was a running list of over twenty names. Each was still legible in that a heavy ball-point pen had been used for the writing. After every name was a phone number and then further to the right on many of the lines were insignificant comments indicating the number of times Trance had talked to, or tried to reach, each of the people.

Cookie took the paper and inspected it. Having been out of the music loop for a while, and having never been a fan of hip-hop, she didn't recognize the names.

"Either of you know who these people are?" Cookie asked the sibs.

"They're all rappers, that's all. Must be guys Trance was getting together with for a gig," Marvin answered.

The names included Beat Up And Down, Count-MeIn, Flip Side, Blue Angel, Luco Bratzi, My Fair Lady, Bumpkin, PityPotty, RiotAct, DumbedDown, Phat Chance, DoughSexEz and a few others the brother and sister didn't recognize either.

"I think I'm going to be busy for a while. I hope I don't wear out that welcome at your parents' home."

Cookie's apartment building had been undergoing rehabilitation after several residents had reported pulmonary symptoms due to mold. The Williams parents had lots of extra rooms and had offered to have Cookie stay until she could move back to her place.

"I doubt it. Cookie, you'd have to know my parents but you have a better chance of them adopting you than kicking you out," Wanda assured her.

It was a different experience for Cookie, a real home. If she was back in time for dinner, she'd eat with the family, case closed.

"I'll keep that in mind. It's so nice of your mom and dad." Then she chuckled as she examined the list a second time from the back seat of Marvin's Lexus. "Weird names," she finally commented incidentally before poking fun at her ex-beau. "And by the way, I don't rate the Rolls Royce?"

"I'll have to wait and see how your bill works out first," he bantered back at her.

"Don't worry about a bill. My payment is getting to the bottom of what happened to Trance. And don't change the subject. Where's the fancy car?"

"This buggy will do me fine," Marvin assured her. "Besides, I've got a couple investment opportunities I'm considering that will pay off a lot better than an expensive car."

"Good for you. Now tell me about these bizarre names." Awaiting an answer, Cookie reached in her purse and pulled out three See's Suckers, handing one to each of them. "It's my mad compulsion but don't tell anyone. I'm now a pure vegetarian—hah, hah. Analysts like to call it an oral fixation and it may be, but I love these. I brought a whole box for your mom and dad and they're sucking on them like kids on jawbreakers."

"With what they're going through, they need it," Wanda lamented.

"About the names. Lots of the rappers are tough boys," Marvin answered while unwrapping the candy. He held it up to his mouth. From Cookie's perspective, the sucker shrunk to half its size next to his huge features. "They want to make a statement with their names. That's about it."

"Yeah, but My Fair Lady?"

"This is Detroit. You know as well as anybody what we're like. Nobody wants to give us credit but don't we have our own standards for innovation? My Fair Lady is a gay rapper; he's hot, Cookie."

"Okay. I'll take your word, Marvin." She bobbed her head, trying to shake out the perceived ridiculousness of the name. "My Fair Lady for a gay rapper. That's got em' all beat."

"Let me say something off the subject of gay rapping or rapping in general," Wanda injected while placing her See's sucker in her purse for later enjoyment. "Trance was a unique sort of boy. He had this gift of being able to get on with anyone. At the same time, he was his own person. He never felt the least as if he had to do like anyone else. I don't believe he had an enemy in the world."

"He had one, we're pretty sure of that, sis," Marvin reminded her.

Cookie already knew that. She freely ran her fingers through the orange-toned strands of her short hair. She was deliberating what moves she was going to make next.

"I have to apologize," Marvin interrupted her silent contemplation. "You keep asking us to tell you everything even if we're sure it's inconsequential. Well, I think I screwed up. I just remembered but right after my brother was killed and the police issued their pathetically deficient report, I received a call from Mr. Fairbanks, the owner of my team. He was very supportive about Trance and said that if I needed anything to call him. I told him that I didn't trust what the local police were telling us. He gave me the name of a man here in Detroit to get in touch with.

"I did. He's a police Lieutenant in a different division but agreed to meet with me, unofficially. He couldn't get any information on the case but did tell me about the department's concern with drug-related crime in the area. He surmised that perhaps how the department was handling illegal substance cases had something to do with the nonchalant attitude I was getting about my brother's case. That's it."

"What's his name," Cookie demanded.

"I can't tell you. I swore I'd keep him out of it."

"I don't give a damn what you promised," Cookie roared. "We need an inside person to help us and I'm telling you as sure as we're all sitting in your car that there is some reason the police are lying. This might go all the way to the top. You're letting me handle this, god damn it, so don't hold out what might be an invaluable ally."

Cookie was talking to a man two and a half times her size. He was stammering to answer back to her—no wonder they broke up.

"We could get this guy in trouble," Marvin meekly commented.

"No, Marvin, this guy might save the lives of other individuals like your brother. If the law enforcement people are covering up, then this is something big. Believe me. Here's a simple point. It is so elementary that I was able to learn it in school. With organized crime, murder comes in cartons."

"I'll talk to him, okay?"

"No, we! I'll talk to him alone. Trust me, I have a better chance by approaching him myself." Cookie made her point. She expected a meeting with the mystery Lieutenant, and immediately. "If you both would be kind enough to take me back to my office, I have my work cut out for the next few days."

Cookie was referring to her bedroom at the Williams' home where she had set up her temporary headquarters since it was easier than traveling back and forth to where she worked with O'Keefe. It was a quiet ride back. Cookie wasn't going to back off, but she wasn't a fool either. She knew that in a situation like this she would potentially be putting her own life on the line.

She wondered why it thrilled her. It gave her a feeling that she couldn't recall ever experiencing even as an entertainer. She remembered a conversation she had shortly after she placed her license with Mr. O'Keefe. Expressing to him similar sentiment about her new career, he offered his perspective.

"You're just doing what you do best. A person can't have better fortune than to find that one thing that you do better than anything else in the world." O'Keefe hesitated but then decided to publicize his thought. "I used to be that way and used to feel blessed that I found my groove. It didn't last forever...so keep that in mind, enjoy it."

"I am, I truly am," she replied.

Marvin and Wanda dropped Cookie off at their parents' home. Her car was parked across the street and she paid no attention as she went into the house. Ms. Williams greeted her with a hug. She invited Cookie to sit and talk for a moment. Cookie was resting on a sofa facing the bay window looking directly on to the front of the yard, and then beyond to the street. Her car was in direct view.

That's when she noticed a police squad vehicle pull up behind the car she was driving. There were two officers seated but they didn't exit. It was only a few sentences into the conversation with the grieving Ms. Williams that Cookie noticed a tow truck drive past the officers' vehicle and then park directly in front of her car.

It was at this point that the officers exited their car. One took out a ticket book and began writing a citation. Noticing the odd circumstance, Cookie excused herself from Ms. Williams and dashed across the street.

"Wait a second, gentlemen. What are you doing?" she politely addressed them.

"This is your car, ma'am?" one of the officers asked.

"Yes. And it's perfectly legal to park here."

"Sorry, but we had complaints from the neighbor's that it has been parked for over twenty-four hours without being moved. That's against—"

"No. I drove it just this morning. You can ask Ms. William who is right here."

"There's nothing I can do about it. We're having the car towed. You're in violation of the local parking code but if you want to dispute this you're free to do so. The instructions are on the ticket. It'll be with the car when you come to pick it up."

In the meantime, the tow driver was hitching up her

car and readying to take it. There was nothing Cookie could do.

The occurrence rankled her. Worse, it raised concern that it was an intentional act designed to harass her. Might it have been a gentle warning by Randolph that she wasn't welcome delving into departmental affairs? After she talked with Ms. Williams, she was near convinced that the gesture was not a friendly one. Her host told her that it was impossible that any of the neighbors would have made a complaint to the police—she was on excellent terms with all of them.

Later that evening, Cookie made random calls to two names on the list, CountMeIn and Bottom Phish. She identified herself as a private investigator hired by the Trance Williams family and wondered if they might have a few minutes to meet with her. Bottom Phish never said a word; instead he hung up. CountMeIn had a different line; she hit a nerve.

"I'm chillix (relaxing) and you jump into my 313 (Detroit area code) with some 730 (crazy) shit. I'm not 808 (police code for infraction relating to noise), am I, bitch?" he shrieked.

He then abruptly terminated the one-way conversation. After the two calls, Cookie was convinced this would be an interesting investigation. She called Marvin and asked where she could get a rap dictionary.

CHAPTER 8: WALLS OF OPPOSITION

When Cookie rose the next morning, she did her full yoga routine and went out for a jog. She then arranged for a ride to where her car had been impounded. She paid the fee and went back to the Williams home. After she showered and dressed, she took the list found in Trance's pocket and made more calls. She was able to reach about eleven of the men and the single female. In each case, the responses were similar to what she encountered with CountMeIn and Bottom Phish. If she weren't dismissed immediately, she'd be jived in circles and then hung up on.

While she was unable to arrange a single interview, as she mused about the poor reception she was receiving, she was able to draw an early interpretation: These individuals on the list were in some way strung together and there was a person or group pulling their strings. Whoever that might be had forewarned them about Cookie being on the case and cautioning them against talking with the intruder.

As she further contemplated the odd situation, it became all the more unimaginable to her. These were not giant stars in the entertainment world, but they were performing artists. She knew first-hand that as a group they were known to be independent, eccentric and imaginative. How was it possible that they would permit themselves to act like puppets? Yet, that was exactly how they were behaving.

She made a few notes summarizing the calls and her early understanding. Then she took off for a meeting she'd scheduled; she'd been looking forward to talking with Chief Eric Randolph of the Detroit Police Department as much as shoveling snow. The appointment had been set for two that afternoon. It was understandable that she didn't anticipate her encounter with The Chief would be particularly cordial, especially after the car caper the previous afternoon—an incident that she concluded had to be courtesy of Randolph.

She had called Randolph's office twice previously to get a meeting but he, like Garland, was not inclined to return her calls. After a third attempt with his secretary informing Cookie that he was in but wouldn't be able to take the call, she lost patience. Once again, she was on the phone with Norman Springer.

"Good morning, Mr. Springer. How would you like to do me another favor?" she asked.

"If it means shoving a hot rod up Randolph's rectum, I'm in," Springer responded, but without the humor one might expect. The man despised Randolph, sensed something corrupt about him, but never had the proof.

"He won't take a call from me and I want to see him about the Trance Williams case."

"I don't own the man's calendar but I can make his life miserable and he knows it. One of my good friends is Pat Shelly. She's a leading city council member. She hates him as much as I do. Let me call over there."

An hour after speaking with Springer, Cookie answered a cell call. It was from Lavender Bruce, the personal secretary to Randolph. Bruce notified Cookie that she had a meeting with The Chief at two the next afternoon.

When Cookie left the William's home, the brightness of the morning had retired. Scattered dark clouds looking like scouts were leading an infantry of more densely packed dimness on an easterly march across the sky, an indomitable force heedlessly erasing the soft blueness that had marked a triumphant clear fall morning. Cookie looked up, shrugging off with a smirk the gloomy, foreboding signs that nature was sending.

Her thoughts concentrated on a series of admonitions she was rehearsing so as to avoid revealing anything to The Chief that might alert him that she was suspicious he was intentional withholding information on the murder of Trance Williams. Likewise, she was reminding herself that not directly confronting him with the insult regarding the car incident would be the best strategy.

She had set her goal for the encounter more generally: introduce herself to the man, and let him know that there was now an outsider looking over his shoulder. Sure, she might dance around the car issue, see if she had the opportunity to poke her thumb in his rib, let him know she was on to his tactic, but only if it might be to her advantage. Most important, her aim was to assure him that he was not dealing with a tenderhearted lady that was easily blustered, browbeaten or bulldozed.

She parked and looked across at the historic structure in front of her. Contrasting with many metropolitan police headquarters housed in modern buildings, the City of Detroit had as recent as 2010 purchased a rectangular-shaped grayish-brown brick property in Greektown for the new-old home of The Department.

She went up the elevator to the sixth floor and turned right to Randolph's office. After being greeted by the woman who she presumed was the same lady that had earlier called to notify her of the appointment, she was immediately taken in to The Chief's office.

Randolph was sitting at his desk engrossed with his computer screen. He didn't look up, nor did he stand to shake her hand. After close to thirty seconds, he swiveled around ninety degrees in his chair to expressionlessly glance her directly.

Cookie was first impressed that his face from a straight frontal view was nicely shaped, with evenly balanced features. Then as he rotated his head left and then right, as if working out a kink, she noticed a disturbing asymmetry of the eyes, one that raised the prospect of a wily character. So distinct was the unevenness of that single feature that she wondered what it could mean… how it came to be.

She speculated that the left eye was an example of a facial element crafted by The Divine Maker using perfect logic and mercy; anyone looking at the man from that side would have had to enjoy a sense of peace, trust and confidence. The right eye, however, dropped as if the man had just suffered Bells' Palsy. It was half closed. It stood at a forty-five degree angle camera shot. From that vantage point, it seemed to be delivering a wink, a shameless notion that eerily threw the entire face into a menacing glare.

Cookie continued processing the inescapable facial flaw. While doing so, she couldn't help pondering another point. How many people had ignored his right-side appearance, reacting to this deviant creature in the wrong way, and paid a price? She cringed, wondering what acts of horror might have been committed by the owner of that mug, a face permanently signaling an unmistakable warning of dire consequence to anyone thinking of crossing it.

"You found us without too much difficulty, I assume," he stated dispassionately. "We're quite proud of this little place, if I may brag for a moment. You see The City bought the building recently from the MGM Grand. It had been a casino for them. If I might add a piece of history about this structure, it was an IRS Data Center before that."

"Interesting lineage, isn't it?" Cookie quickly reasoned. "First, it's a symbol of fiscal discipline due to being part of the IRS, then it shifts to an operation of money by chance, and then…well, what are the monetary options for this latest tenant?"

"We're a public servant operation. We really have no authority in the arena of funding so you may have hit a dead end in your thinking," he grinned victoriously.

"Chief Randolph, we know of circumstances where money becomes a central theme for a public institution…isn't it called corruption? All we have to do is read the newspaper to find ample examples involving elected and appointed officials bilking the system."

As the words rolled out Cookie bit down on her gums, punishing herself for a fruitless confrontational infraction.

"Ms—"

"Cookie, please. My last name is Acosta."

"Cookie, you'll find our department operating with

the highest degree of integrity. I understand you have no prior experience in public governance, but municipalities like ours are not permitted to operate like printing presses." Randolph's lips squeezed tightly, if anything, exaggerating the cunning of his flat stare. "Oh, no. We have standards of accountability here. I hope during your…is this your maiden voyage into investigating?"

Cookie laughed uncomfortably, words spontaneously jetting out she wasn't sure were playfully devilish or simply plain stupid. "I like to think of my maiden voyage as the time I lodged a screwdriver into my brother's abdomen after he tried to beat and rape me one too many times."

Randolph's right eye came to attention; it opened wide, for the first time his face appeared aligned—she realized that one way or another, for better or worse, she had unmistakably caught his full attention.

"I can promise you'll have no need for hand tools on this assignment. All I ask of privately employed investigators is that they don't violate the rules of conduct we adhere to and that they don't get in the way of my people doing their jobs."

"Chief Randolph, I can assure you I have no intention of stepping outside the law or trying to assume responsibilities belonging to your officers. I don't believe you'll find me an offender."

"Well, now we're getting to know each other."

Randolph winked his left eye. "So, since you asked for a meeting, what is it I can do for you?"

"I don't have a laundry list of requests just yet. What I thought I might do is stop by for the purpose of making an introduction. I'm sure you know I was asked by the family of Trance Williams to take a second look to be sure no stones went unturned in investigating their son and brother's demise."

"Good word selection, demise," Randolph popped in like an applause. "Yes, I think it's particularly hard for loved ones to accept the death of a family member that involves either random circumstance—as appears to be the case with Mr. Williams—or dubious behavior by the deceased themselves, especially when their own misdeeds, drugs or crime obvious examples, likely account for their passing. Either way it's not untypical for them to seek a more…soothing explanation for their grief, don't you agree?"

"I've begun my employment in this case with precisely the same line of doubt you're raising. I suppose if the end result is that Trance, for example, were to have been a drug addict and died as a result of an overdose, or, as your department concludes, was killed innocently from a drive-by incident, I'll be in the unfortunate position of having to confirm your findings to the family."

"As I believe I said, no doubt your assignment will be brief."

Randolph was wearing his dark blue officer's suit,

five stars running down the shoulders of the jacket and a silver-DPD pendant pinned on the top of the left lapel. A seven star badge across the top on the left breast announced his title, CHIEF. The word POLICE was beneath it in bold letters. As he lobbed his last word, "brief," he thrust himself forward in his chair, a gesture signaling he'd fulfilled his obligation to see her and if she had more on her agenda she should get on with it.

"Well, it's been great meeting with you, Chief Randolph; kind of you to take the time out of your busy schedule," Cookie responded with forced earnestness. "I hope you're right and I can move on to other matters soon." She hesitated before concluding. "Along the way, I'm sure there'll be a couple of silly nagging items so I'll feel free to contact you, if that's agreeable. You know how it is I'm sure, being an investigator you never want to leave one of those loose ends dangling."

"I understand. I've been in your shoes many times. Good luck, Acosta."

I've been in your shoes many times.

Cookie said it was the moment he made the statement that a bomb went off inside her head. She vowed she was going to extend her investigation of Chief Eric Randolph, not restricted to his role as chief and the possibility of corruption, but to be expanded to include who he was and where he came from.

She'd later comment to me on this single phrase uttered by The Chief that somehow it signaled to her that something was amiss. In her words: "There was a lie begging to be told on his evil face." She delivered her statement like a promise.

I've been in your shoes many times.

Cookie said she repeated his pithy statement over and over, each time with stronger conviction that lurking behind it was an ugly falsehood.

What he said seemed pretty benign to me, but I didn't have the instincts of a great murder investigator, an appellation Cookie was determined to deserve.

CHAPTER 9: BROTHER LOVE

Brownsville, Texas is the southernmost city in that state. It rests about ten miles from the Gulf of Mexico, near the tip of the Rio Grande River. The famous waterway begins its southern journey in Colorado and ends at the Gulf, along the way forming almost 2,000 miles of the border between the U. S. and Mexico—it's the second-longest river in the United States.

When water is plentiful, the mouth at the gulf can suck up ocean-going ships like plankton trapped by the baleen plates of a whale, and then swallow those vessels as they're digested into the navigable channels heading first west and then north. But due to plundering of the precious juice that defines a river, by greedy farmers on both sides of the border, due to the river choking on a proliferation of plant material and weeds, and as a result of nature's unpredictable droughts, the river can get tapped out such that only a trickle is left by the time the oft mighty waterway empties into the Gulf.

Gil Randolph worked for the Port of Brownsville as a cargo inspector. As he gazed out to the south, he calculated that it was at most fifteen feet across the river to Mexico. He recalled only a few decades before sitting at the very same spot where he was now eating a sandwich. Often his father would bring him to play in tiny coves at the bank of the great river. The Rio Grande then would be a hundred feet across and flowing faster than a man in a hurry to see his sweetheart.

Gil didn't worry that the dismal conditions of his cherished river might threaten his job security. The port was active as it received ever greater shipments of steel from the north that would be loaded into rail cars and trucks bound for factories in Mexico.

His sorrow for the state of the river was purely nostalgic. The waterway had been the daily headline story during his early years and he lamented it might not ever achieve its past glory. But more disturbing to him this afternoon as he swallowed a mouthful of a turkey sandwich on white bread his wife had prepared for his lunch was his family. He wondered where he'd gone wrong.

When he was growing up, Brownsville was nowhere near the thriving and expanding city it had become. The border between his beloved country and the southern neighbor was permeable. Often he'd cross over to see friends or for entertainment. Matamoros, Tamaulipas,

Mexico hugged its side of the river as did Brownsville on its side. They were sister cities, the two populous areas entangled inextricably in commerce and human relationships.

At eighteen, Gil Randolph fell in love with Rosalinda Lopez Flores, the most beautiful woman he'd ever set eyes on. It was a burning hot attraction from the moment they met one another at the Club de Regatas, across the border from his home. The courtship lasted only a few months. They wed when Rosalinda was only sixteen. By the time she was nineteen, she had given birth to two boys, separated by eleven months, Eric and Louis.

It wasn't unusual that two brothers born of the same mom and dad would look distinctly different from one another. Eric was of average build and had a light, sandy-colored bush of hair, similar to his father. His skin was flesh-colored, picking up most of the white genes of the couple. Louis, to the contrary, had black hair that was thick, heavy and straight; his skin darkened to closely match the tone of his mother.

That two boys so close in age would be rivals to one another was also not untypical. But as they went on in years, into their pre-teens, it was evident their brand of sibling animosity was classic: The boys each fought with different weapons, Louis' the more lethal.

Eric from the start—the older of the two—was a quiet and docile type. He had a strong curiosity about anything that had to do with nature and the sciences.

He excelled at school and would proudly bring home report cards demonstrating his mastery in math, English and science. His citizenship marks were exemplary. This earned him the respect of his peers who repeatedly supported him in leadership roles, such as class president or representative.

For Eric Randolph the weapon of choice was goodness. He could spin a continuous yarn of it as well as his brother could demonstrate never-ending acts of cunning, deceit, dishonesty, hostility and even violence. Louis was known as a bully, braggart, fighter and wrathful young boy who took pleasure punishing friends and decimating enemies—his favorite target was his brother.

Any chance he had he would taunt, threaten and beat him. Big little brother Eric would innocently subordinate himself to his younger brother, obsequiously submitting to his demands with hopes he'd gain favor in the sibling's eye—he had a scientific mind but was a psychological ignoramus to the extent that he failed to recognize that human temperament and disposition are nearly as immutable to change as creating new elements by bursting atoms. No strategy worked to make peace with his brother. Often Eric would come home with a bloody lip, a head wound whereby after being socked in the gut or face, he'd fall over and hit a stone, or a shiner in the right eye—Louis was left-handed.

At lunchtime the day Gil was eating his sandwich, he was particularly upset because the evening before Louis, who was sixteen at the time, had picked up a kitchen knife and was aiming it at Eric's chest when Gil interceded to stop the assault. What provoked the attack was that the older son, seventeen, rejoiced after opening an acceptance letter from Yale University for the fall semester.

Louis was sickened as he witnessed the scene. He watched as both his mother and father, overjoyed that their child, a boy coming from a working-class home, celebrated the great honor bestowed on Eric. The threesome was fantasizing about the grand future awaiting Eric, when the attempted violence erupted. Foiled from harming his brother, Louis ran out of the home, taking refuge in the back alleys he was becoming more comfortable in than the house where he had grown up.

It was not only the streets that allured him. While Eric had been sealing his future to become a physician or chemist, Louis was setting down roots to become a notorious ruffian. He was perfectly suited to the role, not only by nature-given character but also through his family heritage.

Rosalinda Lopez Flores was born in Matamoros, one of seven children, all girls but one. Poncho, the only male child, was the eldest of the clan. While Mexico would be bickering with its northern neighbor about water rights, labor agreements, chemical treatment of crops and threats to estuary areas that provided natural nurseries for shrimp and marine life, Poncho was slowly, and violently, building one of Mexico's strongest drug cartels. Many opposed the drug trade because it was argued that it took resources from projects that would be more gainful to the citizens of the communities. Poncho's specialty was eliminating the dissenting voices of these adversaries.

When young Rosalinda married Gil and moved to the United States to begin her family, she retained close bonds with her parents and sisters. She was aware that the enormous wealth the oldest son was amassing was being freely filtered to her parents and younger siblings; the whole clan was enjoying life styles they had never imagined living. But it was only Rosalinda, the second child in birth order, and the one who knew the brother best, who refused to take a penny from the notorious Poncho. She avoided being in the debt of her sibling who she realized was dangerous and could bring trouble to anyone associated with him.

While she shared her children with the rest of the family, she went out of her way to preclude Eric and Louis coming under the influence of Poncho or his people. She even declined attending family affairs when the man she referred as the "the venom of the family" was present.

It was predictable what would happen. Louis was infatuated with his uncle. He'd sneak away when he knew Poncho was visiting his grandparents or one of his aunts across the border. Then, likely to spite the one sister harshly judging her brother, Poncho would go out of his way to ingratiate himself to the boy he'd proclaim to be his favorite nephew, honoring him with the name "El Grande Nino," or "The Great Little One."

While Eric was earning his way into Yale University, El Grande Nino was buying a ticket into the world of narcotic trafficking and its cousin, murder. It's impossible to know with certainty if his career as an officer in a criminal network began before he made the attempt on his brother's life or after. It is fact that by the time he was nineteen, he owned bragging rights to the murder of four men, a service he proudly performed for his adored uncle.

Gil and Rosalinda Randolph would finally sadly disown their youngest son, going to the tragic extreme of never letting his name be brought up in conversation between them or with anyone else. As far as they were concerned, they had one boy, a son who would make them proud of what they had accomplished as parents.

As far as the quadruple murder was concerned, the matter was brought to light in an article in the Brownsville Herald. The story read that a man they called "el halcon," (the hawk) had led a cell loyal to Poncho but had been discovered to be talking with people from a rival cartel in Mexico. His birth name was Carlos Arbetas and he and three of his soldiers were found in a black stretch Chevy pickup, each having been machine-gunned with enough bullets to melt down the metal and build a lawnmower.

According to local authorities, two men were responsible for the slaughter. A witness whose name was withheld used the term "gruesome" to describe the scene. She said she recognized one of the men as a fellow she had gone to school with, giving the name of Louis Randolph. An investigation was underway but as of the time the article appeared, no arrests had been made.

After the episode, El Grande Nino, Louis Randolph, disappeared—he would never be heard from again. Two years later, Gil Randolph would tragically die when a cargo container slipped off its platform and crushed him. Grief-stricken, Rosalinda, having suffered Crohn's Disease from her teens, began to have severe alternating attacks of diarrhea and vomiting, passing away during emergency surgery for her illness.

Eric Randolph, the sole known representative of the family, would graduate from Yale University and subsequently complete his doctorate in biological engineering. He would then take employment as a professor at the University of Texas at Brownsville, The School of Public Health.

Up to that point in his life, he had not put in a single day in any capacity in law enforcement, nor would he have professed to have a smidgen of interest in the field. Yet in just over a decade, he—Eric Randolph—would become Chief of Police for the Detroit Police Department.

It's said that during the average lifetime we can expect to have the opportunity to pursue several careers. The human psyche is known to go through developmental phases whereby huge changes in interest, needs, desires and stated goals might occur. These titanic shifts can transform an individual such that they may inwardly and outwardly appear to be different persons.

The question in the case of Eric Randolph was whether or not as a result of metamorphosis, the type of gross re-definition of orientation toward career that seemingly took place was conceivable.

Cookie mentioned to me that as she put the story together, with the assistance of family members and friends she had interviewed as well as newspaper articles and other forms of documentation, she was chewing over that same question—it was one that would challenge both her intellect and instinct.

"Benny, what I was piecing together about the background of this man was mind blowing for me. How could it have occurred that this science-oriented man all of a sudden gets a bug up his...that he wants to become a cop? Did he grapple with the impulse all along, believing he had to do something to counter the type of evil his brother represented? I must have asked myself these sorts of questions a million times.

"I admit the research I had conducted had been

initially based on a rather wild instinct-driven quest on my part to dissect the history of Chief Eric Randolph—and I'll admit as well my motive at the time incorporated a wish to avenge the treatment he directed at me and more so the obvious cover up of Trance's murder. Yet regardless of what prompted me to dig into his background, was I now to believe that the man with a tilted evil eye turned a radical corner at some point? Even more confounding was my questioning how I might have deduced…no, sensed, from one simple sentence—*I've been in your shoes many times*—that something was wrong with the man. I wasn't that good at my trade at that moment—I wasn't even good."

Cookie said she was stumped. She turned to her boss, O'Keefe, to solicit his opinion. He couldn't make sense of it either but had a friend who was a retired psychologist that did profiling on criminal cases for the FBI. He lived in Virginia. O'Keefe called to arrange a phone consultation for Cookie.

"I explained to Dr. Bajwa the whole story, at least what I had uncovered up to that point. I'll do my best to quote him though I'm doing so based on my notes—he was much more detailed than I could ever explain"

"It seems likely, Ms. Acosta," Vijay began, "that the scientific Eric changed his game plan for life after the shameful news was released that his brother was a suspected mass murderer, and then on top of that after losing both of his parents—all these events took place within a short span of time if I'm getting the story right.

"Assuming that to be the case, we might put together a rough analytic interpretation. When certain types of individuals are subjected unexpectedly to multiple traumas in rapid succession these people are prone to go through an experience of 'ego-shattering', whereby after the psychological process is completed a totally different person is born, one that might have vastly different traits and interests than before the crises. If so, it might not be shocking to discover that forbidden elements of the prior personality sneak into the new psychic structure."

"That sounds highly pathological," Cookie commented.

"Yes, it can be. The new character patterns might, in fact, live beside the old personality, a phenomenon we all find intriguing, multiple personality. There are numerous variations on that theme but in answer to your statement, typically when this sort of slicing and dicing of the character structure occurs, it results in what we would refer to as a deviant individual. I'd propose that as the most likely explanation for how Eric goes from academia to law enforcement without visible conflict."

"My Lord," Cookie cried out to me as if it were the moment of the actual revelation. "The right eye is the battle scar, the living proof that what there is now was preceded by something entirely different. The left eye, of

133

course, is the artifact of the past hanging around to keep alive elements of his history resisting burial."

As an aside, in the end both Mr. Bajwa and Cookie would be proven to be totally off track regarding their analysis of Chief Randolph—rather than a psychoanalytic consultant the novice investigator would have done better with an exorcist.

Eric Randolph was going to take her to the brink of mental confusion —she had a whole lot more research to do before she would come to a full understanding of what happened to turn Eric Randolph into a law enforcement official, and what she was sure was a corrupted one as well. That said, by the time she'd met with Randolph and then completed her exploration of the family's past history, she was becoming a more confident and skilled practitioner.

Her efforts to discover why Trance was murdered were taking her in several directions at once. While she was lacing together data about The Chief, she was also scraping for other leads. She knew from the police report exactly where Trance's shooting took place. According to their records, there were no witnesses. Sure, that's conceivable, but always in a case of this sort somebody would later come forward with evidence, even if completely fictitious and motivated by factors unrelated to the crime being investigated—there were no documented instances of this either.

Cookie decided to canvas the neighborhood, drop in

and talk to the people who were likely in their homes when the incident occurred. She busted up The Department's no hitter on her first stop. The material she collected from that single interview exceeded what she'd glean from talking to all the other families close to where Trance was killed. By now, it was November 18th.

The man's name was Gabby Hollins. He resided with his wife and daughter. Her first impression was that she was talking with a dull, simple-minded man. She sized him up as the type that she expected would be easiest to get information from because he tended to be childish and, therefore, by her estimation, likely to run at the mouth the second he was offered the opportunity to be listened to.

"You're already the third person coming out here to ask about that boy getting killed."

"The third, Mr. Hollins?" Cookie exclaimed.

"That's right, Miss. Right after it happened, the detective asked me about it and I told him exactly what I saw. Then a few days later, two men came to the door asking the same sorts of questions, said they were friends of the boy who was killed. Now, you make number three."

"Would you mind going over it one more time? I'm sorry but I'd like to hear from you—"

"I sure will," he rushed to assure her. Then he hesitated on a thought. "Hold on now, I lied. Hate lying. Told my kids from day one not to lie. Like my Momma said, lies are hard to remember because God-fearing people aren't supposed to not tell the truth. So when the lie comes back to them, they don't know what they said the first time and end up being punished for it. I'm not sure I lied to you just now…no, I think I forgot."

"I think so too. But tell me what it is."

"The detective came back a second time…he did. That's when he told me I wasn't to tell anyone else what I saw. Told me it was best I only talk to the police, said people would make things very hard on me and my family if I didn't keep quiet."

"I'd still appreciate it if you went over the details with me."

"I can't afford to get in no trouble over this, Miss"

"Mr. Hollins, I hate to do this to you but you just said, 'I sure will,' committing that you would talk to me about it. So if you refused to now, which I know is your choice, you would have lied to me."

Hollins started laughing. "That's a truth, little lady. I owe you this one."

"I'll make it easy for you. Let me give you my word that I'll never mention your name or us having talked. This will between you and me only. I don't lie either. My God can be a monster taking no pity on cheating and lying."

Cookie had her own views on faith. She considered her God to be a force she could only know from within her own being. Nevertheless, she had tested indiscretions on Him or Her in the past and didn't like the outcome.

"Okay. Then you come on inside so nobody can see us together."

Hollins led her into the living room and asked her to sit. He made a grand performance of his story.

"See, I was right here looking at the paper when I heard the shots fired. I move a little slower now, as you can see, so it took me a minute to reach the window. Well, I notice a human figure on the ground bleeding terribly. Then from right down the block, just a short way comes another man. This other fellow runs up to the fallen one. As he looks down, I might have thought he recognized him. He fell onto the ground with him but he had to know there was nothing he could do to help.

"That's when it happened. The one that was bleeding reached out his arm and slung it around the other man's neck and pulled him in. I could see he was whispering in his ear, seemed like it was a few seconds. Then I heard a shout. I looked behind me. My wife had to have seen the person bleeding from our bedroom and came running in to get me. I turned around and she came up to me crying. By the time I turned back, the fellow was dead and the man who was sitting with him was holding him in his arms in a dazed state. A second later, the siren comes down the block."

"By any chance would you know the name of the man who came on the scene of the murder?"

"I really don't. Wish I could tell you but it was dark and with my wife upset and all...funny, when I mentioned it to the detectives that came by they never asked me if I saw anybody else."

"Do you know the name of the detective who came out from the police department?"

"Don't believe I ever got it, no, don't recollect it."

"And the other two men, what about them?"

"I didn't invite them in for tea, you can be sure of that."

"Something unusual about them?" Cookie pumped the questions as quickly as she could. He was loose at the mouth but her gut shouted that once this witness paused he might realize how much he was revealing and then clam up.

"Just that the one who said nothing reminded me of a miniature version of Mike Tyson, the fighter. Mean looking man. Come to think of it the one who did the talking had a way of threatening you without saying it."

"I have a favor to ask of you. I promise you again your name will never come up in conversation on my part. Would you permit me to come see you one more time, with an artist who could draw pictures of the people you're talking about?"

"An artist rendering. I see that all the time on TV."

"Exactly. It would help a lot if I had an idea who these

people are. I want to find out who killed Trance Williams—that's the boy's name. I also want to stop those same people from killing a lot of other people. Mr. Hollins, you can help."

Hollins stood up and lifted the right pant leg. The entire shin and calf was disfigured, likely the work of several bullet wounds. As he displayed his gory-appearing lower extremity his eyes watered.

"I don't talk about it much, rarely even with Mildred—don't like to think about it. Don't like to especially now that I have my children. That's what I got for helping a stranger. That's why I didn't come out when the boy was shot. Sometimes, it's better to mind your own business."

"I understand," Cookie responded softly. "But Mr. Hollins, if this were only about one man's life, a man already dead, I wouldn't ask this favor of you. Other people, innocent young ones, might be killed if we don't stop this."

"Call me before you come. I'm usually home. But like I said, I couldn't help you with the man who was with the boy because I couldn't see him but vaguely."

Hollins walked Cookie to the door. She looked back to shake hands with him, reminding herself not to forget how dumb first impressions can be. He didn't look as childish as she initially perceived him.

The next day she came back with an artist and left with three renderings. She had now added material to search out a few more liars, ones unfortunately without conscience. These were the types whose job description included murder.

CHAPTER 10: MEETING BENNY WRIGHT

Cookie stayed in close contact with Marvin. While she saw Trance's parents daily, and frequently the siblings would stop by, Marvin was point man. In spite of the fact it was during the football season, he came home periodically and handled affairs daily from wherever he was practicing or playing a game.

Most investigators develop an individualized style. In Cookie's case, one defining characteristic of her approach was her inclination to keep the masses of information she might assemble on a case to herself. She'd been warned by O'Keefe of the risks run by operating in too high a level of isolation, but Cookie had her reasons, especially in terms of sharing her findings with brother, Marvin.

Out of love and devotion, she worried he might go

off half-cocked, placing him or others in danger, or in-advertently hindering the progress of her investigation. Thus, she'd share incidental material with him. Still, she found ways to keep him involved, feeling that he was making a contribution. First, she nagged him to arrange for her to meet with Lieutenant Ian Rosco, his inside contact at the Detroit Police Department. Then, after moaning to Marvin that none of the people on the list found in Trance's pocket would talk to her, she asked the big man to use his influence to coerce one of the artists he knew best, Blue Angel, to meet with her.

Marvin had met the rising star several times and was aware how Trance had admired him. Why Blue Angel, along with the rest of the entertainers on the list, was resisting meeting with Cookie was a mystery Marvin wanted solved as well. Sure, Blue Angel's stock was ris-ing, but that was no excuse. Knowing it never hurt to have the top quarterback in the country on your bud-dy-list, Marvin was confident Cookie would soon be chatting with Angel.

In fact, it was the afternoon of the evening when Garland had scheduled one of his famous "Who's Who" parties when Marvin picked up Cookie to transport her to Percy's Place in downtown Detroit. She insisted on seeing Blue Angel alone. He was waiting for her at a ta-ble. She had no problem recognizing him even without having ever seeing his picture.

No doubt the mother of Lamont Brooks had called

her beautiful boy "Blue Angel" a thousand times. So accurate was her assessment that as he grew up the appellation had to be picked up by the schoolgirls. While few claim to know what an angel looks like, especially a blue one, Cookie said she might have made a healthy bet after seeing Angel from across the room.

"He had perfectly rounded eyes that were opened wide, as if inhibition was an impossibility," she reflected on her visit with the hip-hop star. "His skin was translucent and you could see beams of light shining from deep beneath the outer surface of his being. His plain persona spoke to innocence and benevolence. I wanted to see a halo of colors circling his head. As I stared, my fantasy expanded. Were those white wings fluttering against a deep blueness surrounding him? Were those flowers floating like snowflakes around his essence, laying down a carpet of red, pink, orange and yellow petals for him to recline on?"

"I guess you saw an angel," I quipped after she described her first visual of Blue Angel.

"I doubt it," Cookie sneered. "Once he opened his mouth, I knew he was rotten. I'll bet the Barbie Doll collection that I never had as a little girl that lots of young ladies have learned the hard way that angels not only have wings but talons that can squeeze the heart out of you. Benny, I didn't care for him from the start."

"Haven't you learned your lesson about first impressions?" I needled her, referring to Cookie having

143

moments before told me about her quick judgment of Hollins.

"This is different; trust me," she confirmed with a bobbing of her head. "I mentioned casually to him that I was having trouble getting some of the people in the music field who knew Triple-XXX to talk with me. The conversation took off from there."

"You probably had a stretch of bad luck," Angel replied dismissively.

"I can't imagine that being the case," she challenged, "because even when I tried to reach you, I was rebuffed."

"Lady, I'm really busy. I have a new album I have to cut in the next month. I just returned from a three-week tour. If I could help you I would. The truth is I don't know a thing about what happened to Trance. I'm not going to dispute the police report because I have no cause to."

"When was the last time you saw Trance?"

"Oh, hell. It was quite some time ago; had to be two months at least before he died."

"Did you know anything about his personal habits? You know, like did you ever hear him talk about using drugs or being involved in anything edgy?"

"I didn't know him well enough that I'd feel confident to comment on that."

"Of course, you know you're lying to me?"

Cookie said she had no reason to hold back with Angel and decided to press hard on the pedal, accusing him without proof. Her assertiveness was based solely on a hunch, as well as being sure she had but one shot with him.

"I know you want to stay out of this. But by holding back like you are, you're telling me a lot more than I think you want to."

"I'm not telling you a thing, lady—"

"My name is Cookie."

"Well, Miss Cookie, you know shit about me."

"That's where you're wrong. I know as I'm talking to you that you keep biting down on your gum. People that don't have something to hide don't do that." Cookie reached out and put her hand on his arm, attempting to infuse the confrontation with a gesture of friendship. "You're trying to run like a scared child. Why? I can help you get this off your chest."

Blue Angel's tan-toned skin was darkening. Hostile platelets of blood rushed to the surface, turning his aura purple. His jaw tightened murderously as he stood; his body was quaking.

"I have an attorney and manager. You ever want to talk to me again, get in touch with them—do you know who I am?"

"I'm beginning to find out. You're no angel, that's a fact."

Angel made for the door, nearly spitting saliva on his words as he departed. "Up yours!"

Marvin had been seated in his car waiting for Cookie.

He told her that when Angel came out, he made a quick right and immediately took out his cell. In an instant, he was talking furiously to somebody.

Cookie conveyed the story of her meeting with Blue Angel to Marvin. He laughed in disbelief. "You used to be such a soft spoken woman...except with me, of course," Marvin joked. "I like that sauciness and that willingness to bite into rawhide. It suits you. I just hope I have some friends left after you've finished your work."

"Friends?" Cookie balked. "I have a boy we all loved whose been murdered...and believe me more are going to follow. I don't need friends. Besides, I'm about to piss off a lot of people. I'm hoping one of them is going to help us, even that this 'angel' will think it over and surprise us with a conscience—I won't hold my breath in his case."

The lady then retired for the evening to formulate details of her work for the next few days.

On the top of the list, was yours truly. She wanted to talk with me, pick my brain to see if by chance my prior association with Trance might aid her with a clue, a lead to somebody that might help that was not already on her interview list of artists refusing to meet with her. She wondered if I might be able to shed light on why they were avoiding speaking to her.

We agreed to meet at Jimbo's Bar. When I arrived, I was aware that Cookie still had no idea that I had been at the scene of the murder. Marvin had not only advised me not to come forward to the authorities but he failed to inform Cookie of the fact. Thus, as far as I was concerned on the day we met, only Jewel, Marvin and Detective Howell were aware that I had watched Trance die.

It was eleven in the morning, opening time for the not-so-famous tavern. The date was November 20th.

For a neighborhood saloon, Jimbo's was a joint with a dignified feel, one that Cookie always admired. The interior was mostly crafted from several varieties of wood. Most outstanding to her eye was the bar itself. It was toward the rear of the large room. It was long, and it arched at the ends to abut the wall.

Cookie said the bar top was beautiful, the chestnut wood accented by a marbling pattern reminding her of a prime Spencer steak. The rest of the structure was mahogany and had intricate detail. There were racks above for hanging glasses of varying shapes and sizes, and numerous drawers. The back was mirrored and covered with bottles of hard liquor.

It was apparent to her that the owner took pride in maintaining his business though the floor, composed of planks of dark walnut, showed wear and tear visible even with the low illumination. The inside was painted a tan color but around the perimeter of the ceiling a thin strip of orange accented the otherwise plain walls.

It was the sort of place that most of the patrons returned to over and over again, never considering that

the charm and allure was intoxicating, blending perfectly with the spirits. I was at the bar talking with Jimbo,
when Cookie entered.

I hadn't seen Cookie for several months although her
involvement in my earlier ordeal had left us on good
terms. Jimbo's didn't have much of a female following
so any lady walking in would generally attract attention
from the customers. When she arrived, I did glance up
at her but since she'd been experimenting with endless
combinations and permutations of her physical presentation, I honestly didn't recognize her at first. It wasn't
only the hair that was subject to rapid redecorating, it
was her entire attire that threw me off.

She was wearing a pair of designer jeans formed
tight to the body with a black knit top. On her head,
she donned a Panama derby hat with a wide brim. Then
to top it off, she had on these oversized dark shades.
She was always a sizzling hot lady but she would have
passed for a starlet rather than an investigator. However,
on second thought, I wondered if she had in mind to use
her outfits as a ploy to squeeze admissions out of thugs
and hustlers or seduce general information from guilty
husbands. If so, she was guaranteed to succeed.

We sat down and I bought her a tea. Strangely, I felt
I hardly knew her, or that I was meeting her for the first
time. I felt awkward and she must have sensed it. We
small-talked for a while. I was sipping a cup of coffee

and was about half way through, when she finally poked into Trance's murder.

"I'm sure Marvin told you I'm handling the investigation of Trance," Cookie began.

"I know. I guess we're all broken up. He was an innocent—"

I couldn't finish the sentence. Just like that I broke out crying. I'm not talking about a trickle. I made a damn fool of myself, balling buckets right in front of her. "I'm sorry. All of us who knew him well understood what an amazing young man Trance was," Cookie expressed. "His loss has hurt a lot of people."

"It's not only that," I informed her, while wiping my face like a small boy.

"I understand, Benny. Maybe we should talk another time."

"I really have nothing to offer anyway to tell you the truth. I just can't imagine anyone gunning him down... like a massacre." I stopped for a moment because I was visualizing again the spraying of bullets I alone had witnessed blasted into Trance's body—plus the similar violent event I'd fortuitously witnessed years before. The outpouring of emotion was heedless in the sense that it might have clued Cookie that I knew more than I was expressing, yet at the same time it was an involuntary response that was evoked by revisiting unresolved trauma.

Cookie stood up as if she was preparing to leave. Then, she hesitated.

"Benny, before I go would I be asking a lot to show you a picture," she mentioned as she was reaching into a briefcase she had laid on the floor next to her chair. "There are lots of people here inside and outside of the music industry I need to meet for this investigation. I'm not sure of all of their names. If you don't mind, do you know who this man might be?"

She took out a picture that I immediately recognized as that of the police officer that was at the scene when Trance was killed—it was the face of Detective Dick Howell, an image I'd never be able to forget.

When I saw the drawing, I remained silent. I might have looked as if I was unfazed but what I experienced inside was pure, raw panic. At that instant, several questions blew at me, like a sand storm pitting the windshield of my mind. Most notable, and the one I couldn't help but repeat over and over, was why on earth was she showing my Howell's picture? I simply couldn't imagine.

While I remained staring blankly at the rendering, I was rehashing the events that transpired the evening of Trance's murder. I remembered being struck by the fact that not one person left their home to come out and see what happened. Then, it had been no more than a minute before this unmarked police vehicle cruised up.

Out of the car, had come a single officer. He was wearing civilian clothing. He flashed his badge at me and seemed hardly interested in what I had to say. All he wanted to do was get me out of there as quick as possible, like his mission was to assist me to not be involved. That was it.

As I replayed the scene in my head, I surmised, that at a minimum, he would have questioned me over and over and then he or his associates would have followed up with me the next day—I couldn't get past the fact that I never heard from him or anyone of his colleagues with D. P. D.

"Benny, have you ever seen this man?" Cookie asked again, interrupting a stream of thought that was quickening my pulse. "It's just a drawing but if you've ever seen the man I'd like to know," she asked while still holding the drawing based on Mr. Hollins' impression.

"I've never seen him," I answered sharply, my heart pounding like a rock drummer beating his instrument. "No, not even familiar."

"Well, if something does come to you later, if you think of anything about Trance that might help, call me," Cookie instructed.

She then took out a business card and proudly handed it to me.

"You know the number, but aren't they cool cards?"

"Really cool," I complimented, examining the oddest calling card I'd seen.

It had a dull silver tone with black print. There was a vague figure of a female viewed from the rear, but on the back of the head were two eyes. I wasn't in the mood to laugh but the obvious message was: word-to-the-wise,

I-have-eyes-in-the-back-of-my-head. The imagery did strike me as humorous.

"I'm happy for you, Cookie," was all I said.

Later, I'd learn that she never had any intention of showing me the rendering of Howell. The reveal for her was those few words I had used to describe Trance's murder. I had characterized it being "like a massacre." How could I have known it was a massacre? As I feared, my uncontrollable weepy outburst to Trance being murdered had given me up as a cheap fake: Cookie was quickly learning her craft.

It was a massacre. The police report, however, concluded a shooting took place but never released details for the public. Cookie was certain that I had not talked to the family regarding the particulars of Trance's body, though they were aware that the boy looked like an overused target at a shooting range after taking far too many bullets from a pair of M4 automatic rifles.

The question for Cookie was when to approach the subject with me—when to do to me what I deserved, expose me as the fibster I was. Her instinct was to wait, and it proved to be a wise choice.

CHAPTER 11: ZEROING IN ON SOME BAD DUDES

As she had insisted, Marvin had arranged for Cookie to meet alone with Lieutenant Ian Rosco. He was an old-timer with the Detroit Police Department. His career began in the late 60's as a junior officer. At the time he was introduced to Cookie, he was both the third oldest and longest serving officer on the force.

He refused to see her anywhere near the Northeastern Precinct where he was assigned, instead arranging for her to come close to his home in the suburban area of Melvindale. Cookie had arrived early and was sitting in her car reading a book when she noticed a vintage bright red Sunbeam car pull up in the parking area. She'd never seen the model; it was a leftover from about the time Rosco was a kid.

He had the top down and was wearing a heavy coat.

He hopped out of the car. Marvin had described him so she recognized the officer immediately. Rosco was a trim man who at sixty-seven years of age looked in excellent health.

Cookie exited her car at the same time and walked over to introduce herself.

"I love that car," she complimented. "Flashy."

"Right. It's just the type the police look for when they're in the mood for a ticket…but I have that beat."

"I guess you do," Cookie concurred, assuming incorrectly that he was talking about the fact that as an officer he would be excused from minor infractions.

"No, the way this baby putters along it would take me a country mile to get it to exceed the speed limit," he joked. "Come on. I'll buy you a cup of coffee—or tea if you prefer."

Rosco started talking as they walked toward the coffee shop located in a small strip mall. "All these years and I never thought of retirement, at least not until I began to witness a deterioration of ethical standards for our officers. Things were so bad that in 2000, the city, our own city," he stressed as he motioned for Cookie to sit at a round table, "asked the United States Justice Department to investigate our police department.

"Dear—I hope you don't mind me calling you that but you remind me so much of my daughter it seems natural. I'm aware of the politics involved; you know, inviting an outside agency to take a close look inside your operation is strategically better than having had it forced on you. Still, any way you look at it, there had to be big problems.

"Probably at the top of the list was accusations of excessive force and violations of human rights. What's interesting is that we've got a huge black population in our city but we also have an overwhelming number of black officers, not to mention that most of our upper command members are black as well—only about a third of the officers are white like myself. Yet the complaints roll in, mostly against black officers.

"The outcome of the Justice Department investigation was absurd. Detroit used the findings of the outside agency to trim millions off its budget, cut the force by about a third, and trim down the number of precincts. We're grossly understaffed, underpaid, and of course, overworked. Now, you didn't come out here to listen to me berate my employer but I thought a tad of history might be helpful."

"Lieutenant Rosco, I need information. If you can help in any way toward getting an answer as to what really happened to Trance Williams I'd appreciate it."

"You're disputing the police report findings?"

Rosco had a full head of grey hair with no recession or thinning. It was wavy and he wore it fairly long, allowing him to rub his hands through it whenever something seemed to stump him—he and Cookie shared that same pleasure. However, his query regarding the investigation by his department into Trance's case was with notable sarcasm.

"I'll level with you," Cookie expressed. "The facts I have indisputably contradict what the police are concluding. I know beyond a doubt that the report is an ugly fabrication. There has to be a reason. I'm not the most experienced lady at my work, but I'm not an idiot—"

"I'm retirement eligible. I'm not looking to take unnecessary risks. But if I can assist you without jeopardizing my future and my wife's, I'll do what you ask."

"Take a look at this rendering," Cookie suggested as she pulled a picture from the satchel she had resting on her lap. "Do you recognize—"

"Of course. His name is Howell, Dick Howell," Rosco winced as he took a deep breath. "This is not where you want to go."

"What do you mean?"

"Young lady, I'd hate to see you get hurt. I've seen lots of people with strong convictions, honorable people trying to do good, in the end have their reputations smeared, their careers destroyed and if they weren't wise enough to back off, their lives terminated."

"I appreciate the concern and I'll take it to heart. But what is it about this man?"

"We've had bad cop issues in the past, cops on the take or ones who are willing to go the extra step to satisfy a dirty chief by doing something illegal, immoral or violent." Rosco shifted in his chair and took a sip of his water. His skin had a rosy tone and was soft as well as wrinkle free. Cookie recalled being impressed at what an athletic looking man he was for his age. "Three years ago, Chief Randolph came on board. Within a short time, he cultivated a close association—informal of course—with Howell and three other men; I can also give you their names if you want.

"It's a known fact this group of four has been formed into a special task force by Randolph, one that is never mentioned but is feared by every cop on the beat. Myself, I stay away. I'd never inquire about any of them—doing so would earn a sure visit by one or more of the team and that wouldn't make for a happy ending to my career." Rosco paused to think, deliberating if he was going to continue on the subject. "I just can't go there."

"You don't have to. That's my job. I would appreciate their names, if you wouldn't mind."

"As long as you never mention me. Marvin Williams is a fine young man and his boss happens to be my brother-in-law. That's right. He owns the Dolphins. He asked me to help and I will. I need your word on this."

"I don't even know your name, Mr..." Cookie stopped to punctuate her reliability. "If you don't believe me, I work for Mr. O'Keefe who has been in business for thirty years as a private investigator—he has an impeccable reputation."

"I know the firm. Okay, get out your pencil and paper."

Cookie took a small pad she carried from her multi-compartment purse and began writing.

"Dick Howell, you have that one. The other three are Tip Owens, Saul Reyes and Humberto Herrera—we only have a few Hispanics on the force so isn't it odd that two of the four have Spanish surnames?"

"What are you getting at?"

"I'm not sure, to be truthful with you. It just struck me as odd, that's all."

"What can you tell me about them?"

"Cookie, for what it's worth, do you see how I live as an officer of the City of Detroit? Look around you. It's all middle class for miles. Decent neighborhoods with nice schools where our children play baseball, football, basketball and soccer, parks where we go to walk and jog and on the 4th watch a fireworks show, and giant malls for weekend shopping trips. I'm not complaining. It's the life I chose and generally I've been content that I worked at a profession that...can be honorable.

"Now if you're going to be bullheaded and go against my advice, which I can tell you are going to, you might want to look into how those four men live. I've not done so but as you can understand when the boys chat, which we all do, occasionally one might innocently mention for example that Herrera just purchased a new Porsche or Tip Owens moved out to a home in a nice area in Farmington Hills.

"I don't want to draw conclusions. A man can spend

his salary—or any amount he can borrow based on his salary, his inheritance or stock profits—any way he wishes as far as I'm concerned. The real question is how these guys are affording the lives they live—each of them. Shoot, for all I know they have printing presses. That's where I'd begin, though, if I wanted to know more about this notorious group," Rosco declared. "I'll tell you something else, don't plan on meeting them at one of the precincts."

"Why?"

"Cookie, the remarkable thing is they rarely show up for duty. No, these guys are on special assignment under the direct command of The Chief—it has to be that way."

"Lieutenant, I really appreciate—"

"Just don't get yourself hurt. I know you think you're a tough kid, been through a lot. I can see it. I've been around enough to have an instinct for sizing people up. But I'll promise you this is different from what you're used to. It's one thing for a parent or acquaintance to disappoint or hurt you, another for a top brass to deem you an enemy and want to strike you down."

"I'll keep it in mind. But one other thing before I go." Cookie had two other drawings courtesy of Mr. Hollins. She took them out of her case and held them up for Rosco's inspection. "What about these two men? Have you even seen them?"

Rosco studied the faces carefully. Instinctively he balled up his hand with his right thumb pointing at them. He repeated the gesture as if he were daring his mind to produce an answer. "I've seen them—together. Damn, it's killing me. Don't you hate it when you can't place something? Probably not a problem for you but wait and see when you get older," he quipped.

Cookie took out copies of the originals. "I had extras made. Would it help if you took those and then if it comes to mind, you can call me?"

"Good. I'll get it," he tentatively proclaimed. "Remember, please, be careful…I mean make damn sure if you try to move against any of these people that you have sure backing by at least the FBI. I'm not joking."

Cookie stood, readying herself to leave but before she could turn, Rosco grabbed her arm.

"I've got it," the officer proudly announced, slapping both of his palms on the table. "Two bit thugs…well, four bit thugs. They work for a guy named Mejia. I can't recall the first name, but I can easily get that for you. I suspect they're enforcers, collectors of debt. There's a lot of drug traffic in this city." Rosco leaned back in his chair and smiled wisely. "Automobiles and drugs are big industries, but the one we really should be proudest of, know what it is?"

"Not really," Cookie answered unenthusiastically.

"Thought I was going to say sports? We've had some great ones—football, basketball and baseball. Al Kaline still lives not far from here…you probably don't even know who he is," Rosco laughed.

"Well, now that you have my tongue hanging out to know?"

"Who Al Kaline is?" he teased.

"Well, that too. He can't be on the Tigers…I watch most of the games so I'd know it."

"You're a fan of the Tigers but you don't know Al Kaline? Shame on you," he kindly admonished.

"Shame is right," Cookie agreed. "I was brought up here and I don't know Al Kaline, plus I guess I don't know Detroit's top industry."

"Well, let's start with baseball. Kaline is to the Detroit Tigers what Babe Ruth is to the New York Yankees. The man's a legend in this city. But the answer you're waiting on is…music. That's my favorite enjoyment. All the talk in music is about how the coasts set the trends, but I don't buy it. It's our soul that gets transported east and west and then they repackage it and act as if it was their property from the get-go. It all begins here; believe me—jazz, swing, big band and now hip-hop and rap; all home grown in the Midwest region."

Cookie respectfully listened to Rosco lecture on what had to be a pet topic of his. Having been in the music field for so many years, she took his perspective as a compliment. Whether or not she believed his conclusion was another matter. Frankly, while it was an interesting question to consider, it was of no interest to her. She now had leads. The investigation was taking shape.

"Thanks again, Lieutenant. I would appreciate it if

you could send me the first name of Mejia as soon as you can."

The following day more names would be added to her list of suspects needing to be investigated. Javier went with Mejia. Then under Mejia she wrote the names of the two thugs Rosco provided for her: a slightly built, lanky white man named Anthony Wilson and a muscled black brute going by the name of Roland Turner.

CHAPTER 12: MR. O'KEEFE, I NEED YOU

John O'Keefe kept an unusual schedule. On a typical workday, he'd come into the office between nine-thirty and ten in the morning. He'd make a few calls to friends, balance his checkbook for home and work, and enjoy a lengthy visit to his bathroom, accompanied by one of his favorite Hustler magazines.

His figure was exceedingly thin, an obvious consequence of fulfilling his nutritional needs almost exclusively with the remains of one or the other of his favorite brews.

His scalp shared with Lieutenant Rosco the same thickness and waviness with no sign of recession, the latter a miracle given O'Keefe's ritualistic habit of meticulously combing it backward from the forehead for almost sixty years. The private investigator's hair color, however, varied in that it retained a rich auburn tone. His skin reflected his Irish heritage, a rosy complexion that required sustained spirits early after arising in the morning to perk up.

Cookie had in mind that, under the surface, he was pained, yet the man would have argued vehemently that he was living the best years of his life. He had a live-out girlfriend he saw when in the mood. Male relationships were abundant. At least twice a week, he'd take in a round of golf with his cronies, at least double that number of evenings out of seven he'd spend several hours at Murphy's Pub watching sports with drinking buddies (all of his associates were drinking buddies), and when he had the opportunity, he'd take in a ballgame of one sort or another.

What made his life all the more pleasant was that he had a full professorship providing a nice salary, permitting him to not have to worry about billing hours for his business. Now, as Cookie was taking on more of the cases, he was reducing his duties all the more. Even with some neglect of his practice for a few years before taking Cookie onboard, he still enjoyed a solid reputation, a fact that resulted in plenty of work for his new assistant to expand her experiential base.

Thus, by noon most days he'd leave the office and take off for lunch, usually never returning until the following day.

During the relatively short amount of time she'd

worked for him, Cookie found O'Keefe to be an invaluable ally. He was eager to teach her as much of what he'd learned over the years as possible, plus he was agreeable to assist her in the cases he was delivering to her.

She quickly learned that while he was not willing to engage in illegal actions, he was agreeable to crawl up to the line demarcating ethical, moral and legal approaches from their less prestigious cousins on the other side.

"Cookie, there's a vague border between what we define as ethical and what is not. There are times when you'll have to linger cunningly at that hair-thin but identifiable partition separating right from wrong. Then, on occasion, you'll need to turn it into a four-lane highway upon which you can race and zigzag on journeys to destinations far beyond your wildest definition of legal or ethical. This is not work for the meek and faint-hearted," he'd caution. "Just be sure you wear a crash helmet when you're speeding," he'd laugh.

O'Keefe offered another critical benefit to her. He had over the course of decades, developed a vast network of influential and prominent associates he could call on for literally any imaginable service—the man in a matter of hours could attain information she thought could never be produced.

She was always enthusiastic to learn how he accomplished what he did, and he was more than willing to share his secrets with her. His specialty seemed to be technology. He had a stable of wizards that never failed to provide assistance in any area requested. Almost anything conceivable, from confidential notes on upcoming corporate mergers to home addresses and personal data on congressmen, senators and celebrities, could be accessed—for a price.

"Let me give you some advice," he'd counsel his protégé. "You'll learn everything you need to know about your clients—for that matter about anybody that comes into your life—if you pay attention to how they handle money. Some think it's essential to make a gambling trip each month to Vegas but will plead for time to pay your bill because they're broke. You'll have clients that will pay you a ton to spy on their wife but won't put up the funds to help their children get through school. I love the type that want their service for free because they think you should be blessed to have such a prestigious client…and they know full well that you can't violate their confidentiality by telling anyone that they are refusing to pay their bill—they're also the type least likely to recommend you to others.

"Cookie, it stings to get stiffed so be sure to always take a good size retainer and never deliver the goods until you get full pay—I'll be here for a while to show you the ropes. And above all, be a straight shooter. Charge your hourly fee and bill for every nickel of expense but always give them a detailed accounting of ancillary services. If you know you'll need to employ vendors, provide the client an estimate beforehand, and never add a percentage—you'll find that the more sensitive and complex the information you need, the more it'll cost. And don't forget this either: You can buy most anything, but not a fine reputation and honor."

Immediately after talking with Lieutenant Rosco, Cookie called her boss.

"Mr. O'Keefe, its Cookie."

"Where you been? Haven't seen you in days," he said merrily.

"I'm handling that murder matter I told you about for a friend...the freebie."

"Community service. Did my share of it as well. Never hurts to give."

"This is a little different," Cookie explained. "It's going to be time consuming right now. Also, I might need your help with backup matters."

"Of course. Just let me know what and when."

"I think some of this will have to be handled with utmost delicacy."

"Delicate? That'll cost you," he howled, speaking to her from Murphy's.

Cookie recognized the familiar sound of loud television screens in the background and understood that her boss had retired for the day. Still, she was always amazed that he could drink from sun up to bedtime but never seem inebriated. To the contrary, she found his mind sharp regardless of how much spirit he was consuming. It was known fact that he'd lecture while intoxicated;

yet he'd still be able to entertain the students with case studies, scientific material and personal experiences as lucidly as if he were sober as a puppy.

"If this isn't done with complete confidentiality, I might be in trouble—"

"Don't want to lose my best investigator," he continued with jocularity.

"Nor do I…Mr. O'Keefe, I've made a sacred commitment to living."

"I'll ditto that. Don't want to put the brewers out of business."

"There's going to be quite a bit of work here, so let's take it piece by piece. I don't want to break my client."

"I understand."

"I'm going to give you five names. They're all here in the Detroit area and employed by the Detroit P. D."

"Dirty coppers. You sure you're ready for this?"

"No, but I'm all in."

"I've had a few instances dealing with law enforcement personnel. You have to be very careful," O'Keefe advised paternally.

"I'll let you know if I'm in trouble."

"Don't get in trouble; that's better. Now, I doubt it should be too costly getting basic profiles. Let me see what I can do."

"I appreciate it, Mr. O'Keefe. I'll explain the details to you when this is over but these clients are good people…and grieving. Anyway, what I want is addresses and as much personal data as you can get. I also need you to have their bank accounts accessed. I want lists of deposits and withdrawals for the last three years—details on where the deposits came from and where the withdrawals went," Cookie listed like a take-out food order. "When whomever finishes this job, it's very important that what they did disappears—"

"Like a fart in the wind? You're getting smart, lady."

"Thanks, really."

"When do you need this? Sometime this evening okay?"

"Right."

"Computers work round the clock. Wait and see."

O'Keefe woke Cookie at midnight.

"I have it all. You have a fax I can access?"

"I set one up where I'm staying with these people: 314 784-2766," she yawned.

"These are policemen? They're each making multiples of what both of us take in together. Better be careful, dear. Cops are nasty bastards when somebody tries to nose in on their drug deals."

"Drugs? I don't see any sign of it yet, but—"

"Behind every financial inconsistency, there has to be sin. Remember I taught you that?"

"Yes, I do. But there are lots of types of sin."

"When cops are involved, drugs are the best bet. Sleep well."

Drugs. Other than the single statement made by

Rosco to Marvin that Trance's death may have been conveniently misclassified in order to mitigate data relevant to a growing drug problem in the city, Cookie hadn't considered drugs because she was sure the kid wasn't a user and wasn't wrapped up in illegal activity.

Drugs, sex, prostitution and gambling always seemed to be lurking in the shadows of corruption, treachery and violence. She'd look over the information in the morning. She was unusually tired, more typically a freak who could go long stretches without rest and still not turn into a cross animal.

When she woke, she picked up the volume of papers faxed by O'Keefe and headed for the kitchen.

While staying at the Williams family home, each morning Ms. Williams insisted Cookie sit for breakfast. She treated her like the youngest child that she still wished hadn't left home. Thus while Cookie was swallowing sips from a cup of green tea and spoons of fresh fruit and yogurt from a bowl, she was choking on the material she was scanning regarding the finances of Howell, Owens, Reyes and Herrera. They were taking in hundreds of thousands over and above their salaries for each of the three prior years, the period of time since Randolph was hired as Chief.

Cookie still had no idea that some time ago Trance's buddy, Happy Robinson, followed a different game plan but ended up at the same place, three separate accounts, all at the Dearborn bank. Trance had seen the money being disbursed for luxuries and as lump sum payments to individuals. At that moment, his primary focus was on assembling the material that would prove that his friend, Rough Diamond, had been murdered. He was aware of the perversions seeping into the music scene in the Midwest but hadn't carried his investigation to its logical end. Had he lived long enough no doubt he would have forged forward to research the identities of the other people—many included in Cookie's list—enjoying fortunes extracted from the end accounts.

Cookie was now appreciating the opportunity to take her investigation a step further. She had at her disposal lots of names, names of famous, and not so famous, entertainers and recording artists that were somehow linked on a list prepared by Trance. Then, she had proof of financial dealings for four crooked cops. Could they all be linked together? She pondered a question that should have been rephrased: How are they all linked together?

After breakfast, she packed up the material O'Keefe had sent her, plus a few cursory notes. She'd decided to take a ride before finding a quiet park where she could work. Her goal was to drive by the homes of each of the four men. It was plain curiosity. But also, she wanted to see with her own eyes if these men were acting with impunity. Was it possible they were making no attempt to hide the illegal revenue they were receiving for god knows what sorts of mischief, likely assignments

171

conducted on behalf of…Randolph…and/or whomever else?

She found that the men had chosen homes at locations that formed the four corners of a near perfect rectangle, for if each of the dwellings were to be pinpointed on a map of Detroit they would show Owens at the northwest corner in Farmington Hills, Reyes in Livinia at the southwest corner, Herrera at the northeast corner in Ferndale and Howell in Hamtramck, the southeast corner.

Their neighborhoods varied but each of the homes they lived in was the nicest in their respective community. Owens and Herrera had older homes in established areas and the other two had rebuilt homes. Each of their properties were immaculately kept up and the visible vehicles were all late model and in the luxury category.

After she completed the last line of the geometric tour of the city, she found an open green-forested park area not far from Howell's home. The fact that these four officers were a lynching squad working under the command of Randolph, and Randolph only as far as The Department went, seemed indisputable to her. But Randolph couldn't afford to be paying them unless he was determined to be a principle in whatever illegal activity was being enforced.

It was more likely that Randolph fell into the same category as his subordinates. That is, he had to have been recruited for his position and then instructed to put together a team of loyal, ruthless and fearsome soldiers to handle special projects—they would all be paid ridiculously well for whatever services were expected of them.

What she wrote in her needing-to-be-done notepad was that she wanted to get similar financial data on Randolph that she had attained on the other four men. She also had to complete her research into The Chief's background. After that, her goal was to get back to O'Keefe and request details on the three accounts from which these four men were receiving their compensation. She also placed an asterisk beside a request to attain more than just the transactional information on these accounts from which the officers were receiving payments. She wanted to know who opened each of them and who had authority to sign checks.

She knew she was getting hot and didn't want to waste time. O'Keefe was still in the office when she called to detail her request for additional information. Knowing confidentiality was a golden rule for her boss, she was confident that the process of attaining the material would never be traced back to her. She recalled a recent case where O'Keefe was asked to do surveillance on a state senator because the politician's wife was certain he was having an affair. When the job was completed, the only person on the face of the planet having access to the findings was the client employing him. Cookie appreciated being able to have that faith in him.

Even under the most favorable of conditions, however, there are times when an investigation could take an unexpected and disastrous turn due not to perfidy or double-dealing, but unavoidable error. Occasionally, the smartest guys get outsmarted; a hair intentionally placed across the opening of a door that is no longer there when the party who planted it returns can be a giveaway to an agent or spy that an unauthorized entry had occurred. There are also invisible security procedures that can be attached to accounts at banks by clients who are highly sensitive to violations of their privacy.

Cookie was going to get the information she requested. She was also going to set off an alarm that would eventually designate her an enemy, an appellation she'd have preferred not being given by the owners of three little accounts at Dearborn-Detroit Savings Bank. Once that happened, there would be no mercy dispensed toward the unsuspecting lady.

In the meantime, she would be busy digging herself deeper into a world of filth. Randolph wasn't impressed with her. More likely, he plainly didn't like her and resented her snooping around his domain. He thought he'd send her a gift, a get-out-of-town kick in the rear present—this was without him knowing anything about her recent findings, including her investigation into his history.

When she left the quiet spot where she had stopped near Howell's home, she went to get her car. She'd left it up the road, parked out of her sight. As she approached it, she noticed the front hood looking crud-colored and covered with something dark. When she came closer a malodorous smell caused her to step back and cover her nose—she might have thought she'd slipped on a bucket of dog doo. The entire hood of the car was smeared with feces. Fingerprinted were the words: GET IT?!

Cookie was more than certain now she was being harassed, and it had to be Randolph. What confused her was how he would know where her car was. O'Keefe had expertly trained her to slip a trail as well as to know when she was being followed—she'd been highly observant ever since she began making contact with people regarding Trance's murder of the possibility of someone making her the object of investigation.

She took a deep breath and held it. Then she lay on her back to inspect underneath the car. As she might have suspected, there was a small sensor, a chip no doubt placed for the purpose of linking her vehicle to the Global Positioning System—Randolph was following her and knew everywhere she went by car.

Cookie took the vehicle back to the Williams home and hosed it off—she was too embarrassed to take it as it was to the rental agency before removing the stench. Once clean, she returned it to the company. Then she arranged for another vehicle that she rented from a geographically remote, small enterprise. She had a set of documents to permit her to operate under an assumed name. She used these to rent the vehicle.

Her inexperience betrayed her at this juncture. Had she reasoned through the situation more carefully, she'd have realized that if the car message had been the work of Randolph, then he would have planted the sensor. The next logical conclusion would have been that he knew that she had driven past the homes of all four of his buttons. She would have been correct to be greatly alarmed. Her strategy then would have dictated her going fairly deep under cover. For the oversight on her part, she was about to lose two rooks and a bishop—narrowly avoiding a checkmate.

CHAPTER 13: AN UNEXPECTED VISIT

By this time, I had heard nothing more from Cookie. I was delighted that was the case. Still, I remained troubled by the meeting with her. The thought that I might be implicated in a murder case, especially of a young man I admired, haunted me.

Jewel had left for work. Both of my children had taken off for school. It was a rare moment when I had the house alone. Typically I'd have been at the plant myself but I was asked to cover a later shift for a friend and agreed to do so. I recall it was November 22nd. The wind was howling. Nervously, the back door was banging in the frame and several pieces of loose fitting window glass were chattering. The house seemed eerie, which only enhanced my sense of disquiet.

I tried to smile myself out of what I knew was a foul

mood. I should have known better—this was not going to be a good day. In fact, any mirth I might have tested would soon be wiped clean from my face.

The festivities began precisely at eight o'clock. I had poured milk into a bowl of my favorite cereal, Sugar Pops. The day before, I'd purchased a small box from the manager's cafeteria at work. Forgetting to have it as a snack as I had intended, I stuffed it into my jacket. Jewel refused to purchase the brand due to its unhealthiness…so I was cheating. I took a spoonful and stared at the walls of our small breakfast room, feeling for a moment the deliciousness of indulging in a harmless act of naughtiness.

Then I heard a knock on the door. When I opened it, two men were staring at me. One I recognized. His presence unnerved me. I tried to swallow the partially chewed puffs of breakfast in my mouth but my throat constricted. The men didn't ask permission to enter. Instead the lead man, whose identity I knew, pushed the door harder than the blizzard force winds outside. The second one followed, as they thrust themselves into the room.

"Saul, close the damn door. It's freezing," Detective Howell barked at his partner.

"Sit down!" the man, who Cookie had shown me a drawing of, ordered. "Do you know who I am?" he asked gruffly.

I nodded, simultaneously mouthing acknowledgement.

"You might be in a lot of trouble," Howell warned. "There's some broad nosing around for that hot shot football hero brother of Trance Williams. She wants to look into his little brother's murder. You know who she is, right?"

I hesitated, not wanting to reveal I'd recently met with Cookie.

"Do not screw with me, Wright, or I will fuck you up right here. Are we clear?" Howell shot at me. All I was able to muster was a second nod of my wobbly head. "Now you met with the bitch, right? So let's have a little talk about what you said to her."

"She did most of the talking," I explained, my voice quivering. "She asked if I knew anything about Trance's murder. I didn't. So I had nothing to tell her."

The other officer, Saul Reyes, lurched at me, grabbing me by the collar. At the same time, he kneed me in the groin. I saw white pain. It bleached my mind's ability to think. Reyes, a large burly man, kept yanking me upward, denying me my instinct to bend over.

"Don't piss me off," Reyes warned as he let loose.

My skin dropped enough shades for me to pass for white. "You were there when he was killed. You're the only witness. Marvin Williams brings her to you and you never tell her you saw him gunned down? You want me to believe that story?"

"It's true," I pled. "I had a similar experience three years ago and I guess I'm still trying to put it behind me. Look, I don't want anything to do with his murder because I can't help solve it. All I want is to be left alone. I never told her. I didn't tell anyone."

I knew at the moment that I was lying again but I deemed it necessary to protect Jewel's safety. She was the only person who knew, well, except Marvin and Howell's people. The last thing I wanted was for my wife to be brought into the matter. Sadly, the boys had their own point of view.

"You know, Wright," Howell drilled at me, "one lie leads to another. We need to get the rules set. You lie to me and it gets me angry. When I get angry, I want to hurt someone. I can't tell you why and I can't apologize for who I am. That's just the type of guy Dick Howell is. Are we speaking the same lingo here?"

As his question was posed, Howell punched a blow upward into my lower gut, knocking the air out of my lungs and leaving me paralyzed for several seconds.

"You never told your wife?" he shouted. "Do I need to pay a visit to her myself to find out the truth or—"

"Okay, okay. Look, I'm just trying to keep the people I love out of this." I was choking trying to draw air to my empty lungs. "She knows nothing except that I was there. I swear there's no more I can tell you. When it happened I was so upset that I hardly paid attention to details."

"See, here's the problem we have. I know you're lying. There's more to the story. I know you didn't do the shooting. But is there anyone else who could prove you didn't? What if it ended up that there was a clue at the murder site leading to you?" Howell was shaking his head as if he was convincing himself it was true. "You could be charged with murder, Wright." Then he glanced at his partner. "I think we might have a piece of evidence. Saul, what do you think?"

"Bastard shot him in cold blood."

"Could be. Or at least an accessory," Howell compromised.

"I didn't do anything. You know that, you were there. You never contacted me afterward."

"Just shut your trap and listen. There might be people who will testify that you had it in for Trance, that the kid was achieving success at your expense or that you had a dispute with him over the delivery of a parcel of an illegal substance. It's not unreasonable to conceive that you had a big fight with him and threatened to shoot him. Did you set him up by meeting with him, knowing that when you told the shooters where he was he'd be murdered?" Howell shouted with such esteem I was I was inclined to buy his fantasy. "Why didn't you come forward, Wright?"

"You said you'd contact me if necessary."

"I don't know a thing you're talking about. You see anything in the records about a witness, Saul?"

"Not a thing, boss."

"I've kept you out of this, Mr. Wright, but if I bring you back to life pertaining to the Trance Williams case you're going away where you won't see that family of yours for decades. Now think about that. We'll be back to see you. It may be an hour or a week, in the morning or middle of the night—we'll be back! Keep it in mind because you can bet on it. That snoop investigator wants an answer to Trance William's murder? We'll give her one. Don't think we can't do it."

"I don't understand what you're asking of me," I cried out. "Just tell me."

"I'm giving you one chance to figure it out yourself and do the manly thing before it's too late. You know what I'm talking about…one chance."

"Trance was trying to tell me something but he—"

"So what was it?"

"Well, he died. He was never able to explain what it was."

"You better get that memory of yours working, Wright."

The sky lit up brightly and then a few seconds later thundered. The illumination highlighted the devil in their eyes.

"I want to know what he said, that's it. One chance!" he spit at me before signaling to Reyes it was time to leave. Howell slammed the door as he exited, nearly smacking it into his associate's face.

I was baffled. Am I being punished? I'm being threatened with what even I initially believed to be a foolish thought, a charge of murder. I didn't have a clue why, nor what these dishonest officers wanted from me.

I racked my brain but still couldn't figure it out. All I knew was I was shaking when they left. Then to make things more exciting, those animals that roughed me up weren't gone ten minutes before my cell went off. It was Cookie. Was some greater force in the mood for a game of let's-see-how-much-stress-it-takes-to-break-Benny-Wright-down-to-Jello, I wondered?"

"We need to have a chat again, Benny."

"Look, I can't, okay. Just don't call here again," I asserted in a fashion I'd have never spoken to Cookie.

"You sound scared, Benny. What is it?"

"I can't meet with you, do you hear me?"

"I do hear you. I have a feeling you and I are going to end up more intimately involved over the murder of Trance Williams than we were for our little caper three years ago. You because you can't get out of the situation you're in, and me because I refuse to."

"I didn't do anything," I whimpered.

"I know that. Just for a few minutes. All I want to do is ask you a question. Benny, it's me. You know I'd never do anything to harm you."

She was right. If there was anyone on earth other than Jewel that had earned my trust, it was Cookie.

"They know I talked to you. God damn it. You want to get me killed?" I blurted out.

"No, actually I want to save your life," Cookie said matter-a-fact. "I'm learning, Benny. Sometimes we get put in situations that are not of our volition but we're forced to play a role. Benny, there are times we can't run. We have to stay and fight. Don't make me chase you."

The last words she said, about staying and fighting, was like a smack in my face. She knew most every detail of what had transpired years earlier when my response to failure was a strategy of flight. Is that what I had chosen again by not coming forward with an admission that I had been at the murder scene? Was I going to continue to run by not telling anyone about Trance's final words, ones that still had no meaning to me? But Marvin told me to stay quiet about it.

"If you're concerned about somebody seeing us together I can deal with it," Cookie promised me. "Benny, I've had the best teacher in the world guiding me. You're going to have to have faith in me if I'm going to help you."

"Can't you just ask me on the phone?"

"Benny, we're going to be meeting more than once. I can tell that's where it's going."

She hung up the phone.

I was bewildered. An hour later a courier came to the door with a message. *Here's what I want you to do…*

Cookie had me drive out to a park nearby in

Woodbridge. It was a small wooded area with a plot of grass and a full playground for children. It's called Bryant Vermont Park. She instructed me to get out of the car and walk around the perimeter. If she didn't come to meet me within ten minutes I was to leave and she'd get back in touch with me. It was real spy type stuff but it made me more comfortable meeting her, and more confident in her. I did as she asked. Within a few minutes of ambling around the outer track of the park, she came out from behind a clump of trees.

"We're safe. Don't worry," she assured me. "You want to know why I called you again?"

"Yeah, I would."

"There are lots of reasons why people lie. O'Keefe told me about a fraud case where the key witness didn't want to come forward because he knew his wife's brother would be headed to jail and she'd never forgive her husband. Lies Benny. There are a thousand reasons for them. The list goes on and on. Not all lies are bad. Some are even heroic or courageous. My job, Benny, is to know when a lie is being told and then determine if it's going to harm innocent people."

"So you're convinced I'm lying?" I asked.

"Yes."

"Seems you're not the only one."

"I have no idea what it is you're hiding, or why. All I know is that if you keep avoiding the truth, you'll be bringing harm to people that had no responsibility for what happened to Trance."

"I don't get the heavy guilt trip you're putting on me."

"Benny, the first innocent person is you. The second is I. As I told you on the phone, I'm afraid we're going to find ourselves bonded in this experience though I can't explain why…not yet. I only know I'm getting close to figuring this out. That's all I can tell you."

"What do you want?"

"Why did you describe Trance as having been…massacred? You used that exact word, 'massacred.'"

"I could have used any word."

"But you didn't. You showed all the signs of a person who'd seen trauma when you said it. Trance was massacred, and you knew it. I think you saw it. And I think you know more. I also think there are people who want to know what that is," she said forcefully. "Now who was it who came to see you? Who threatened you?"

Her question weighed on me so much that I'd lost all normal perspective. In a matter of an instant, Cookie Acosta might as well have been a stranger. I couldn't tell if she was a savior or another demonic force. For some reason, my faith and corresponding sense of trust abandoned me. It might have been Dr. Jekyll standing in front of me and I'd have had no way of discerning if I was facing the good or evil side of his split personality.

"I'm going to go out on a limb here and take a wild

guess," Cookie continued to pepper me. "Was it the man in the drawing that I showed you the first time we met?"

"How did you know?"

"His name is Howell, Detective Dick Howell. Did the other man go by either Tip, Saul—"

"He called him Saul," I responded softly.

"His name is Saul Reyes. Both of the men that came to see you are officers of the Detroit P. D. They work as a team under the direction of The Chief. They're being paid extraordinarily well, so I'm sure you can figure out that means two things: they're involved in illegal activities and they're extremely dangerous. These men can operate like an assault squad, yet with the full authority of The Department. I'm on their radar. Benny, so are you."

Cookie was using a slingshot to awaken me.

"Benny, I'm trusting you, possibly with my life. I need a little back from you."

"What?"

"Tell me what you know about Trance. Why he may have been killed. What you saw that night. Also, equally important, what did Howell and Reyes say to you?"

I told her everything I knew. She wrote down notes.

"Let me get this straight," Cookie calculated. "They're saying that if you don't give them whatever it is they want, which you don't know what it is, they'll set you up as the murderer or as an accomplice? Is that the gist of it?"

"I think so. But it was so vague. I'm not even sure they think I have something or that I said something. It's very confusing."

"Benny, go home. Do you have a secured phone?"

"Just my cell."

"No. That won't do. I'll have a phone set up for you under a different name. When I need to reach you I'll only use that number and if you have need to call me do not use any other phone. Leave your car unlocked tonight. It'll be under the passenger side seat when you go to leave for work in the morning. In the meantime, think like hell what they want from you and why they're so intent on getting it. Benny, they're scared about something and when people like the ones we're dealing with are fearful, that's when they're the most dangerous."

"All I wanted to do was keep living a simple, dumb life. What did I do?"

"Benny, don't make more of it than 'shit happens.'"

"There's got to be a reason."

"Oh really? I've been at the same place you are more times than once, and there was no reason."

"Makes me think about what my friend, Simon, said one time," I reflected. "I'll do my best to quote him."

> *Life seems to be made up of billions and billions of logical and rational events, random circumstances that make up real history, each of our personal histories...and we largely ignore them. Then there's a tiny, miniscule fraction of*

happenings that seemingly are highly improbable, deemed orchestrated by a higher power. These make no sense to us.

Yet these few magical experiences are the ones we spend time dwelling on. Christ, they're so powerful they define the history of mankind. From those scattered statistical infrequencies, events we can confidently predict will occur because the unlikely becomes increasingly more likely as time passes; philosophies and theologies are born, with civilizations and cultures sustained on their backs.

"His final statement summed it all up," I stated.

Man created Gods for the sole purpose of asking protection from those disempowering moments.

"So where do we find a God of Protection?" Cookie laughed.

At least I had the good sense not to ask Howell for an answer.

189

CHAPTER 14: HAPPY CATS AND BAD DREAMS

Both Cookie and I remained in the dark as to why Howell and Reyes had visited me for the little chat. Unbeknownst to us, there was an explanation. Trance's computer had been stolen from his apartment. To secure the contents, it had been handed over to an "expert" in technology hardware working for Mr. Mejia. After two days of fiddling with the machine to try and unlock the code used by Trance to secure it, the moron attempted a forced entry and the machine went into deep cover.

When finally—well over a week later—it was placed in the hands of a competent person, it was a near impossible task to recover the files. Then, to make the task all the more formidable, there were literally thousands of files. Trance was a rebel. He refused to take the advice of the personal computer world and replace his unit at least every five years—he had a machine he'd been using since junior high school.

It was initially reasoned that they could search his computer drive by using the dates the files were established—the job should have been a snap. But when they approached the assignment logically, they came up empty-handed. Because Mejia couldn't afford to take a chance, he ordered that every bit of data on every file be examined. After days of work, they scored a victory.

Had Mejia not insisted on a full search, they would have never found it. Young Trance must have been worried that something untoward could happen to him. What he did to protect against someone breaking into his home and discovering what he was collecting on the murder of his friend was to embed the information he was accumulating in a different file dating back a decade, into a file with a series of short stories he had written.

When the file with the report created by Trance Williams was found, a copy was delivered to the Parra Brothers who took a look and shit themselves—not the sort of information a cartel leader wants his enemies to uncover.

Waging war was the first reaction of Mejia and his people. Then they realized they didn't know whom to battle or even if a conflagration was necessary. One of the cooler heads in a leadership position came up with a brilliant question. Had anyone checked to see if Trance had made a copy of his report? If he hadn't, then the problem might have been resolved on its own. Since he had his own printer, the archival record should show what copies were made recently and of what materi-al. That's when it was brought to Mejia's attention that the thieves who ransacked Trance's office also took his printer.

These men who first entered Trance's place hadn't been instructed to take the printer or backup drive. They couldn't have answered why they did grab both items. Not perceiving the printing device as particularly valuable, they ultimately found a resting place in a pile of junk in the corner of an office in Monterey, Mexico owned by the Parra Brothers. The piece of equipment was later sent out to the same expert who handled data recovery for the computer. He was able to use his sav-vy technological tools to confirm that at a time corre-sponding to just prior to Trance leaving his apartment on the evening when he was killed, he had printed a lone copy of a document of precisely the same length as the incriminating material on the computer—no duplicate copies had been made.

When information has been documented that can expose an entire network of criminals, and then like-ly bring the governments of two countries to wage a counterattack on the wrong-doers, a single copy—the number one—can hold as much sway as a million, a billion, or even, a trillion copies. Knowing that Trance had printed out the evidence established grounds for the Parra Brothers to declare war. The Boys would have smuggled their entire army of soldiers into the United States to fight if not for one thing—they still didn't know who the enemy was.

Howell and Reyes were sent to Benny Wright to scare the proverbial dung out of me. It wasn't as simple a matter as getting me to admit whether or not I had the document as to determine what I had done with it if I did have it in my possession—or for that matter what I planned to do with it.

They hadn't concluded that I possessed it. How could they? All they knew was that I was the only witness to the murder and that Trance had been huddling close to me when he died. This they found out courtesy of the Detroit Police Department Special Task Force of Thugs, but not until much later.

At the time the two men Lieutenant Rosco identified as Anthony Wilson and Roland Turner went to see Mr. Hollins—the neighbor who was first approached by Dick Howell of the Detroit Police Department, and later by Cookie—the communications between Chief Randolph and the Parra Brothers people simply hadn't been completed. That Benny Wright had been at the scene was inconsequential, at least until the existence of the document put together by Trance was discovered. That's when I became a celebrity.

It was the contention of Howell, when he talked with Chief Randolph later in the evening after he met with me, that I knew something. His opinion was to place any amount of pressure necessary to break me down, essentially frighten me that my life, and the lives of my family, were over should I try to get cute. Randolph, however, cautioned his assistant to do nothing until advised by Mejia. He had been told that Mejia was concerned that if I was holding the document, I might have made copies that I gave to people to release in the event anything happened to me. Mejia had a better idea. He was going to meet directly with Garland.

It was Garland's turn to be torched.

*****

Cookie was busy. O'Keefe had been thrust into the role of playing assistant to his assistant, not even fully understanding the implications of the work she was conducting. Regardless, he was feeding her data on an hourly basis.

I was running in circles, terrified, remorseful and confused.

Randolph and his team were sharpening their weapons to go into an offensive mode and rid themselves of an irritant sex pistol investigator along with a lying S. O. B. (me) likely thinking that I could play wise guy and extort money for the information I had fortuitously received. All they were waiting for was Mejia's order.

Garland? The man was just a happy dude. He was getting so rich and powerful he thought it laughable that no matter what he did he ended up bathing in a golden pool. Then one afternoon he received an unexpected visit—the calendar was close to closing out November. He'd still never met Mr. Mejia in person but had received a few phone calls from the man to discuss business. His only direct contact with representatives of Mejia was with his two hired ruffians, Wilson and Turner.

Mejia was a short man with blackish-brown, thick straight hair that was groomed immaculately, matching his style of dress. He wore a black pinstripe silk suit with a lime green dress shirt and black tie. His eyes were covered by dark shades that Garland recognized as Armani, the same maker of the man's suit. Javier Mejia presented himself as the consummate Wall Street financial wizard rather than the cartel general that, in truth, was his title.

Mejia smiled to Georgia who was at the reception desk at the time. He motioned for his two associates to take a seat. He then walked past Georgia as if she were invisible. Garland was on the phone at the time hustling a deal with a Los Angeles record label. He looked curiously at the man who boldly stood staring at him. Normally, Garland would have excused himself from the phone conversation for long enough to tell the intruder to get out. On this occasion, however, his instinct warned against him doing so. This man did not impress Garland as the type to dismiss.

"So we are cool?" Garland said gleefully to the party on the line.

Mejia had invited himself to sit. He seemed relaxed as he took a cigar out of a large brass box sitting on Garland's desk. He fondled it like a joystick before eyeing Garland as if to warn him to cut it short.

"Because we have to be cool with the little ladies," he winked tentatively toward Mejia. "Now you be packin' for a trip to the top. Hah, hah. I'm jetting."

"I don't believe we've met before but I'm Javier Mejia." He paused to let the point sink in to Garland.

Mejia had a habit of punctuating his style of delivery by taking long pauses between sentences, seemingly designed to avoid the possibility that what he had to say would not be received by the party he was addressing. "Now, usually I wouldn't be coming to see you myself but my presence should alert you that what I'll be saying to you is of utmost urgency."

"Whatever you need, count on ol' Garland," he chirped.

"Good. I presume your business is doing well?"

"Couldn't be better. I'm landing top of line people for you."

"I hope our association will thrive for many years. This is an important enterprise for myself and the people I represent."

"I've got ya covered," Garland jived. "Anything you need."

"As it happens there is something I'll ask you to take care of for me. There's a young man I understand you know well. His name is Benny Wright. He's actually a good friend of yours…or should I say…was a good friend?"

"We had a little—"

"What a man does in his personal life or what a good friend of a man does to a friend is of no interest to me. I'm of the belief that Mr. Wright has something that belongs to us. It's of no value to him. But the people I work for, in particular, don't like the fact that he's gaming us."

"He's a straight up—"

"Don't interrupt. These are papers with information that could be incriminating for many innocent people. I'll tell you candidly that I'm not positive he even has them, but he's the only person in my opinion that could. I want those papers," he shouted, pounding his tightened right fist on the table.

Due to the impulsiveness of the frightening outburst, it immediately induced a small bead of sweat on Garland's forehead.

"It's done. Just ask ol' Garland," he responded with an obsequiousness he never knew he possessed.

Mejia glared at Garland. "There are two men who accompanied me to your office. They're sitting outside in your waiting area. They have particular fondness for me. They can't tolerate anyone showing disrespect," Mejia's voice softened. "If I have to invite them in here to teach you a lesson in manners, I don't believe you'll be particularly pleased. I'd suggest you cut the jive crap with me."

How can a man lose about a foot in height in a matter of a sentence—while seated? Garland slumped in his chair and proved it could be done. His smile disappeared and his face turned a frightful dull tone.

"Now what I want you to do is get in touch with Wright. Explain to him that we want this handled peacefully, without anyone getting hurt. If he turns over to us what we want, he can go on his way and no harm will come to him or his family. Understood?"

"Mr. Mejia, could you give me a clue what this thing is so I can be sure he understands?"

"There are some papers I believe he has. Just take care of this because if the content of what he's holding gets into the wrong hands lots of people are going to be taken down, you in particular—and I'll make damn sure it's you first." Mejia tipped his forehead several times to drill the point into Garland, who didn't seem to get it.

"Me? I'm just advising—"

"What do you think is going to happen when it's brought out publicly that most of your clients have been placed in business deals that the government deems illegal? Furthermore, when your name is associated directly with people that are being charged with corruption, murder and a number of other crimes, do you think you'll be exempt from prosecution? I must remind you that we made a sizable investment in you—we're partners now."

"I see." Garland's voice was muffled as he swallowed air. There was no sign of cheer on his face either.

"I think you do. And you can remind Mr. Wright that we can find him, his wife, and his children anytime we want. If he cares to keep them safe, tell him not to do anything stupid. I hope you can explain to him that we're the type of people he'd prefer to have as friends rather than enemies." Mejia took an unusually long time for his statement to register, appearing to be calculating another thought. "Yes, I'll be expecting you to get back to me real soon…a couple days…no longer."

"If I could just ask before you go, uh, yeah, well what if he asks me how you know he has this item. What should I tell him?"

Mejia stood up. He adjusted his firm frame to an erect posture and then used his hands to straighten the lapels of his jacket.

"Tell him we know he was there when Trance died."

His appearance now in order, the boss walked past Georgia and out of the office.

Encounters with people he didn't believe he could crush were not Garland's favorite activity. Meeting Mr. Mejia was a new experience for him, one he wouldn't have even permitted to show up in a dream.

I couldn't believe it when I received the call from Garland. I hadn't spoken with him much. There was little for us to talk about once I had exited the music business. Then when I heard his voice, the tentativeness, the quaking…I just couldn't imagine what it was because he didn't sound like the Garland I knew."

"Benny, we need to talk," Garland entreated urgently.

"What's wrong?"

"Nothing yet, but we might be in a lot of trouble."

"Garland, we…can't be in a lot of trouble. I can or you can, but we have nothing together now."

"That's where you're wrong. I have to see you—real soon."

"I just can't today. I'm working and—"

"I'm telling you not to screw with this," Garland shouted.

"Tomorrow morning," I reluctantly consented. "I'll meet you at nine at Arnie's."

"We need to go over this situation together," he panted.

We did meet the next morning. It was the first time I'd ever in my life seen Garland without a bullshit smile and jolly demeanor. Even as kids growing up, he had a reputation as being the only one of our group who never seemed to be upset. He was the coolest character. All of us as teenagers had to wonder if he was putting us on. His personality veered far off center from where the rest of us were—he couldn't be anything but light, while the rest of us knew the blueness of a moody day.

He wasn't like that when I saw him in the morning. I really couldn't believe it, especially my reaction to him. To see him so morose and subdued, made me think he'd

just bumped into his own superficiality in a dark alley-
way; worse, it appeared that the shallowness and frivo-
lousness he'd engaged perhaps for the first time in his
life had beat the snot out of him—it scared me. He was
shaking and…he even looked frightened.

"So here's the deal, buddy," Garland began in a rush.
"You can have trouble, or you can have a whole lotta
trouble, know what I mean?"

"Slow down, man. I really don't know."

"Trouble, Benny. I mean like with people who aren't
nice."

"You're not telling me anything I don't know, Garland. I've got people threatening me and I don't even
know what they're talking about. Man, I'm like a walking corpse."

"Look, I got myself into a situation that's a little…it's
tricky, Benny. Damn, man. Sometimes things just happen and all of a sudden you're doing business with the
wrong people. See what I'm saying."

"No, Garland. To tell you the truth I never know
what you're saying. Besides, what does whatever you did
wrong have to do with people coming around and kicking the crap out of me for no reason? Yeah, it already
happened. They want something from me. I haven't a
clue what it might be."

"See that's it. They're all the same people. They came
to me too," Garland whined, his voice shaking and his
hands tremulous. "If I don't get whatever this thing is

from you, bad things can happen. It's not only me, but it's also you, Jewel and the kids. We're in this together— we gotta row in the same direction now."

"Just tell me what you need and if I can give it to you, I will."

"The papers, Benny. The papers," he whispered as if the only other customers in the café, two men sitting across the room, might be eavesdropping. "They think you have the papers that can bring down all of these people, including yours truly."

"Where are these papers?" I muttered, even more confused now that I was hearing about them from someone other than Trance.

"Damn, Benny, do you have them or not? If you don't, you got a lot of explaining to explain why you can't explain. I got to get you to these people so you can explain what you can't explain because they're the kind of people who don't take no for an answer."

"Well, I really don't know what to say. Do you have any idea what these supposed papers have to do with?" I asked.

"Trance, Benny! They told me you were there when he was killed. Were you?"

I know that since witnessing Trance being murdered, no matter how hard I had tried to put the trauma aside, I couldn't. It had festered inside me, leaving me in a foggy state of semi-consciousness. Then as time went on and I was approached by Cookie, the Detroit P. D.

roughnecks, and then Garland, I began to shift my attention to figuring out what Trance was trying to communicate to me. I obsessed over every detail from the moment he came calling that evening at my home to when he died in my arms.

I dissected each of his words and every syllable a thousand times, attempting to find a clue that would help me complete the missing message of the final sentence. Read the papers...You'll know what to do... "They're in...

They're in what...where? I kept pondering.

Then, listening to Garland asking for these papers, it somehow connected a bunch of dots I'd have had to be a genius to put together at any prior time. Desperation is not known to inspire people to higher states of mental capacity. To the contrary, the urgent and terrified circumstance of the mind causes brain asphyxiation, a guaranteed formula for logical thought to be disturbed. People typically react impulsively and irrationally, or their mind shuts off completely, when operating out of fright.

There I was, in that unfavorable condition of near hopelessness, yet somehow speaking with Garland all of a sudden I relaxed, for just long enough to reflect on the evening of Trance's murder with a new sense of vision; I was able to execute a methodical examination of the details of what had transpired from when he arrived at my home to when I was holding his dead body in my arms.

Trance had knocked on the door. Then he motioned for me to come outside to speak in private. I suggested we get in the car because it was cold. We had just begun speaking when Jewel called me to let me know Simon was on the phone. I opened my window to tell her I'd call him back.

Trance took off. I followed him. I watched as he was gunned down. I ran to him. He spoke his final words to me regarding the papers, assuring me that I had them. Then, finally he told me that once I read them I'd know what to do.

There was only one point in the progression of events where he could have bestowed upon me the gift.

Sitting with Garland, rehearsing these thoughts from a new perspective, the power outage that had kept me continually in the dark abruptly ended. A floodlight came on. Its beam pointed not in my face but rather into the temporal space between when Jewel called out to me while I was in the car with Trance, and an instant later as I answered her. Then I shifted the dimension from time to physical space, my inner gaze glancing to the now il-luminated inside of my car.

"Yeah, Garland. I was there," I rejoiced as I bolted upward, an electrical force shooting through my body accounting for the physical movement.

"Then you—" he excitedly tried to entice me to continue.

"I gotta go. I'll call you later this afternoon."

"Benny, do you have them?" he pled. "You got to tell me."

"I'll call you."

"Benny," Garland implored, "they want to make a deal, that's all. Just give them what they want and they'll leave you, your family…me, all of us alone."

"I'll call you," I promised him.

I left Garland practically in tears—he was an emotional mess. I had no heart for revenge and wouldn't have tormented him out of pleasure for having once attempted to steal my wife and children. I whisked away from him due to the simple need to validate if my deduction regarding where Trance had deposited the mysterious papers was accurate.

I had taken Jewel's car because mine was being serviced at the Chevy dealer. They must have thought I was on drugs, or at least a madman, when I screeched into the parking lot and then ran up to the service writer handling my car.

"I need to get to my car, right now," I demanded.

"Let me take a look where it is," the man calmly responded. He typed into his terminal and a second later had an answer. "Oh, Mr. Wright, it happens to be ready."

"I need to get to it now…please," I shouted.

I think he didn't want to deal with whatever drama I had brought with me. He pointed in the direction of a large two story parking area. "Stall 286. You'll find it there on the second floor. It's unlocked but the keys…"

I never heard the rest of his instruction. I sprinted to the lot and took four steps at a time getting to the second story. Almost as soon as I hit the top level and entered the parking area, I was looking at my car. It seemed so innocent yet I knew it had hidden within it an answer that could as easily end as save my life.

I opened the passenger door and sat in the seat. Then I scanned the area in the same way that I imagined Trance might have done. I noticed the pouch on the door and I reached inside. That's when I felt a packet of folded papers. I took it out and shoved it in my pocket. Once in my possession I retraced my steps, ending up back at the service writer's desk.

"I'll pick it up when my wife brings me later," I shouted as I ran past his door. "Thanks."

The man stared at me as if I was goofy.

I drove down the block and turned on to a residential street where I parked. I now held the document in my hand that Trance had wanted me to read, the one he presumed I'd know what to do with, the one he'd stashed in my door while I had turned to respond to Jewel, the one he wanted to leave with me for safekeeping in case…the one that he no longer had with him when he took off to be massacred.

I didn't know what was inside it but I had a good idea that it wasn't a recipe for gazpacho soup. The way things were shaping up it was more likely a ticking bomb set to explode my life to dust particles in a matter of seconds, hours, days or weeks.

I finally read the material Trance had written. As I digested each step of the journey he had diligently chronicled, I understood his strategy of furtively leaving it with me. He had no intention of risking me getting mixed up with the criminals he'd uncovered. The only reason he entrusted the document with me was a just-in-case-something-unanticipated-happens last ditch precaution.

He was going home to counsel with his family about what to do. However, he reasoned that if he sensed something was going to happen before he arrived there, he'd want the corruption exposed—he didn't know anyone else he could trust to "know what to do" in case he had to call me to take action for him.

What he expected I would know regarding what to do with the information, or why he thought I'd be able to act on his findings in a constructive manner, I can't answer. All I could think at that moment sitting in Jewel's car after reading the papers, was that I wished Trance would have made it home—I was stumped regarding how to proceed.

At least I understood why these assassins were coming after me. I had enough proof in my possession to cause hurt to lots of people. No doubt if the information were to be put in the right hands, it would set off a domino effect that would implicate a whole lot more people than even Trance had identified.

The knowledge unfortunately didn't seem to be of much value to me. If I took it to the police, I'd surely be killed. If I tried to get in touch with the people threatening Garland, I'd surely be killed. If I said nothing—the same as I'd have to do if I had not found the papers—then I'd likely be killed, and possibly my family as well. I recalled the words of the first dying man I'd witnessed gunned down three years earlier.

"Sometimes we have to do the right thing, even if we die…"

He also failed to finish his last words, leaving me to try and interpret his meaning. He seemed to be conveying something virtuous, suggesting that there are defining moments in life when acting with honor and integrity matter more than life itself. How lucky was I was to have a second existential moment.

I read the material over one more time, grumbling to myself about why my luck was running so poorly.

Rough Diamond had been killed. I wouldn't have believed it, had I not read over Trance's findings. Rough Diamond appeared to be a contented kid who if he used drugs at all, certainly had no cause to kill himself. Then I had to face that Garland was dirty. I knew he was like a commercial vacuum machine sweeping in all the talent in the region. But doing so as part of a scheme to help sanitize dollars for evil drug dealers?

What would have possessed him to get involved with people of that sort? I wondered. He was already a great success.

Greed? Stupidity?

The man's spirit was so thin you couldn't drown in it, but in business he was crafty. If he needed to turn things to his advantage he didn't mind acting with ruthlessness. But he was not a criminal. However, when he came to see me that morning what had to be eating away at him was that his associates and him were going to be prosecuted; the party was about to end for Garland. I understood then that his life was running on as short a leash as mine, the same one in fact.

What did I do with the material? That's the big question, isn't it? Any sane person would have taken a chance on the authorities and had them place my family and me under protection until it was safe. I knew the police in Detroit were as trustworthy as counterfeiters, plus I knew after the visit from the detectives that roughed me up that they were at some level complicit with the parties now controlling the music industry in our central states.

It would have made sense for me to reach out to the FBI or some other state or federal agency. I'm not sure in my jumbled condition that I even thought about it. I'm a guy from Detroit. What do I know from calling the FBI?

Cookie! She was the only person I could think of that might know what to do. So I called her. She never answered. Worse, she didn't return my calls all that evening. I couldn't imagine why—I'd retrieved the secured phone she left for me in my car. However, what I hadn't realized was, that out of habit, I had my personal phone with me while the one Cookie had given me I thoughtlessly left on my nightstand. I didn't even consider that I was using the wrong device.

That error left me convinced that Cookie had abandoned me. I knew her to have her issues but as far as reliability she was as true as a hangover. I panicked; she was the dollar bill, the last currency on the planet with worth, yet for some reason she had forgotten about me, or worse, turned against me.

I knew better than to withhold a story of importance from Jewel but under the circumstances I didn't want to panic her until I had no choice. I knew that nothing was going to happen to me before I reached out to Garland. After that, I'd need to take steps to protect her and the children.

Why had Ms. Predictable Cookie crumbled? Even with me using the wrong phone, she never answered nor did she try to reach me. Why? She had big problems of her own…but that's a story to be told in due time. For now, I'll simply say she was dead on right about her premonition that she and I were going to be drawn together.

Garland? After the disappointment of not being able to reach Cookie, I refrained from calling him. He reached out to me several times but I intentionally re-fused taking his calls, as I concluded Cookie was doing with me—I'd never get back to him.

CHAPTER 15: THE INVESTIGATION CONTINUES

The air was foul in Detroit. It was well into fall. Soft winds wafted the smells of everything from hotcakes in the kitchen to steaks on the BBQs in backyards. One would have expected aromas pleasing to the senses. Yet it stunk. What could account for the odor permeating the city?

There were several people sweating over the prospect of their lives either being terminated or destroyed: there's a unique brand of body stench produced by the glands when fear is the stimulant and there had to be a barrel of terror for each of the keys actors in this drama—a live production that was quickly tightening like a knot on the characters. What a rotten smell.

Even Cookie who was known to always present with a fresh scent was out of sorts. More recently, she had been exuding the confidence that her tangerine, orange, vanilla and jasmine tainted Boucheron fragrance promised. Yet now that she was smack in the middle of muck, her fancy spray bottle wasn't doing the trick. What may have accounted for her malodor—in addition to justified fear—was that she had put on a helmet and shoulder pads and was in practice to beat the daylights out of her opponents.

Cookie's main concern on the morning after I'd tried for the tenth time to leave her a message was that her phone had been put out of working order. At the same time, I was in a panic wondering what to do, doubly perplexed that she wasn't returning my calls after she had pursued me to cooperate with her. At the same moment, she was infuriated to discover that she had never been able to receive my calls. She used Ms. Williams' phone immediately when she discovered the fact, but by then I'd gone out for a walk—with the wrong phone.

With O'Keefe's help, she determined that the disruption of service for her phone was done at Randolph's request—war had been declared and the phone company was fighting on the side of law and order.

While Randolph was confidently running the campaign to defeat Cookie, his enemy was gloating over the astonishing material she had put together on him. She could hardly contain her thrill as she wrote page after page—outlining every detail of the second phase of her research on The Chief—the stupidity of the City

213

of Detroit would never be forgiven. For the Police Department to even consider hiring him for the position, spoke to the incompetence of the public officials overseeing the law enforcement agency.

No wonder the air smelled rancid in the country's auto capital. Randolph reeked. His four henchmen stunk. Javier Mejia, Anthony Wilson and Roland Turner were foul to the nostrils. The stench of the Parra Brothers was nauseating from all the way across the Rio Grande. Garland . . . he'd forgotten how to laugh, which was a stinking shame for him. Detroit was fetid.

Cookie, a posse of one, was feverishly showering her body in cologne in an attempt to cleanse the air. The investigator, still a fledgling, was getting ready to launch an assault on the Detroit P. D. on a level unequaled in the history of the city, and likely the country.

Cookie had already gathered proof that Randolph's people were taking payoffs to perform special assignments as part of a quick response task force under The Chief's direct command. That was old news, and not that big a deal. She had also attained insight into the movement of money. On her own, she'd discovered that artists involved in the scheme were depositing millions in an account called LimeyShadeBlood Enterprises. From there the loot went into those same three accounts that were being used in part to pay off Randolph and his crew—why three accounts, rather than one or two, she never understood except for an off-the-cuff explanation offered by O'Keefe that perhaps it improved the odds that the volume of dollars being filtered through them wouldn't gain attention from financial regulatory agencies.

Regardless of their rationale, it became apparent to her that it was drug money that was being run through a full cleaning cycle and coming out ready-to-spend legal dollars. It reminded her of another drug-related enterprise that had recently been made public involving horses in Ruidoso, New Mexico.

That time it was the Zeta's drug operation, one of the biggest in Mexico. They took a position in racing in several states, Oklahoma being one of them. They had established themselves as legitimate horse racing people and were running thoroughbreds in top stakes races. They ran horse ranches, hired top trainers, and bought great horses at top dollar. They were influencing the entire market for thoroughbreds and driving up prices.

Her case study as a student into that scandal came back to her, as she realized that the process was identical to what was happening in Detroit. The criminals in my home city had set up similar operational controls to those in New Mexico—the only difference was they were riding on the backs of artists. Cookie explained the horse fraud to me one afternoon when she was filling in details of our story.

"Riding?" I object to the personification of my

ex-profession as a musical artist in unflattering language. "Come on, Cookie, we're not animals."

"You're right. I apologize, Benny, for the poor characterization. The way they packed those singers they were mules."

"That's better," I bantered.

"If I have your permission, I'll go on," she said playfully. "I can't wait—you're going to love hearing about my meeting with Chief Randolph, but first…" she chuckled with a lick of the tongue on her orange-shaded lips.

"Benny, I wanted to find out who represented the money behind this organized crime circuit that finally I was able to prove had been responsible for acts of murder—at least two, Brent Calhoun and Trance Williams. I had asked O'Keefe to get me more detail on the accounts. Obviously, if I knew who opened them, who wrote checks and so forth, I'd at least be closer to the answer.

"My boss took care of it with no trouble. He called on his top-data thieves who were good enough to crack through and get the information, but not astute enough to cover their espionage. It so happened that by this time—unbeknownst to O'Keefe's geniuses—the Parra Brothers were already aware (from Trance's document) that Trance had figured out their game. The information Trance had attained could have only been the result of him employing somebody to snoop around the brothers' bank records.

"To counter this, they had installed intricate security procedures for their accounts and business interests around the country. Their records at the Detroit bank were now monitored routinely. So, as soon as O'Keefe's people went in, Mejia was notified that the accounts had been hacked.

"I was still able to find out that it was Javier Mejia who opened and administered the accounts. He handled everything on behalf of the Parra Brothers who were operating out of Monterey, Mexico. The brothers rarely crossed the border themselves. Still, they were using the money to buy up choice parcels of land and residences in exclusive areas around the world. Large withdrawals from these accounts were funding some of those investments.

"Mejia must have gone nuts when he found out that once more someone had been able to tamper with their accounts. The mere fact that it happened had to wake him to the reality that he and his bosses were under some sort of investigation—that discovery by Mejia was made within a day of when I came to meet you, Benny—when I told you I'd be calling on the secured line.

"Anyway, it didn't do much for Mejia, when he finally determined that it had to be me who was tinkering with his toys. Now it wasn't only Trance that had incriminating information on their operation, but me as well. There was no choice but to get rid of me as quickly as possible," Cookie smirked.

217

"They knew I had been hired by Marvin Williams. Randolph had me followed as a matter of principle but not with the purpose of taking direct action to harm me. He would have done so, joyously I'm sure, except when Mejia put out the order to eliminate me, it was sent to his two best agents. Our friends, Anthony Wilson and Roland Turner, received the call and their little caper, which I'll get to in a second, was what sent me packing out of my comfy quarters with the Williams'. I had to leave in order to protect the family members from being innocently harmed.

"Sure, I was being careful all along once I was on to Randolph having me followed. I considered him a nasty brat who wanted to intimidate me but would only go so far without cause. I would have never surmised at that moment, that anyone was suspicious about the accounts being broken into—whatever the Parra Brothers and Mejia had detected due to the bank's security on those accounts neither O'Keefe nor I had a way of knowing. I was casually going about my business without genuine worry that I was in danger. I assumed that what I was doing would make me a target in the future, but at least by then I'd have had time to prepare for my safety.

"Sadly, I was taken by surprise. I had gone out for a jog. On my way back, about a block from the Williams' home, I had a freak accident. Somebody had left a common metal coat hanger lying on the street. As my left foot hit the ground and then thrust forward it slipped inside the loop, and with perfect timing the right foot came down and landed on the backside of the object.

"What it did was stop my left leg from its natural forward movement, the halt so abrupt it sent me lunging sideways from the street toward the walkway. I have to tell you, Benny, that this time I had a bizarre stroke of luck save me. That misplaced coat hanger allowed me to live.

"The fact that I fell onto both of my outstretched hands and then my left knee—log-rolling to the side with my knee badly scrapped and bleeding—is of little consequence. What mattered was that in my striding motion, I hadn't noticed a vehicle far down the block coming toward me, at an increasing speed. As I hit the first step into the wire, I heard the roaring sound of the engine revving. The car was aiming at me.

"I swear I could feel the movement of the air as that car narrowed the space between my shoulder and its left front fender. Had I not flown sideways like a projectile, the car would have done as it intended, run me down. Now, having missed, the driver wheeled his vehicle around swiftly and was coming back for more.

"I'm fairly limber. I had my body do a double tumble to clear myself on to a lawn area. The car, in the meantime, was accelerating. The driver pulled up on the front yard of the house just south of me and was determined to take me out but realized there was no room to negotiate his vehicle between a tree and the house to get a clean shot at me.

"That's when I noticed the two figures. I was sure I knew both of them from the renderings I had the artist do based on Mr. Hollins' description of the two men who came to him to talk about Trance's murder—it was Wilson and Turner. I noticed Turner had a rifle outstretched. He was about to take aim on me. I tumbled again, this time into bushes that were lined evenly along the front perimeter of the home. I heard innumerable shots and saw the stucco of the structure explode in every direction, creating a cloud of debris allowing me to scurry to the corner of the house. I raced from there to the rear yard.

"That's when I jumped fences and made like a rabbit through front and back yards before I was at least two streets away from the Williams home. I was panting and sweating. I couldn't catch my breath. The only thing I could think was if my wish to see Adele live in concert would ever come true.

"I huddled in the back of a stranger's yard, hiding behind a senior citizen weeping willow with growth thickly drooping to the tall grass beneath it. I didn't move for at least a half hour. Finally, I heard sounds from within the house. I knocked on the back door. It was risky because anyone would have wondered why I wasn't at the front. It turned out to be a teenage boy home late because he hadn't left for his job. I asked if I could use his phone and he kindly let me.

"I placed a call to Marvin. He went to my room and emptied out the items I needed: my computer, new phone, purse and clothing. When he arrived to pick me up, I came out cautiously but there was no sight of the two men. Still, I ducked down on the floor of the car as Marvin drove. While out of sight, I looked at my cell. There was a message waiting from O'Keefe, warning me that all the accounts in question had been abruptly closed—he was letting me know that the operation had been detected but his call was too late.

"Marvin made up an excuse to his parents for my hasty departure. I mentioned to him that I needed to go undercover, deeply. That's when he volunteered the apartment of his new girlfriend who by chance happened to be out of town.

"He drove me there and I insisted he drop me off two blocks away in case, by chance, anyone had followed him. I instructed him to not come to see me under any conditions but I would get in touch if I needed him. He drove off and I disappeared. I fibbed to Marvin but it was a precaution I had to take for his safety more than mine. I trusted that he wouldn't betray me but if he panicked he might disregard my admonition and come to the apartment—the untruth was that I decided not to stay there.

"Instead I made calls and found a nearby building

with units they rented by the day that were actually small apartments. I walked there and took a suite under the name of Nancy Winger, the name of a secretary I had worked with when I lived briefly in Ann Arbor. I settled in my new home at precisely the time when... you were desperately trying to reach me, Benny.

"O'Keefe arranged to have fake identification sent to me overnight. The first order of business was using it to rent another car. Then I paid a visit to Garland—November was racing to the finish line; it was the 28th.

"I'd figured out by then most of what I needed to know about each of the men involved in the drama. I had sufficient documentation to fry some big herrings, including Garland. I still hadn't decided what approach I was going to take with these criminals, especially with them aching to kill me."

Cookie looked tired as she was recounting this portion of the story.

"Care for a lunch break?" I queried. "My treat."

We ate heartily and then it was back to work, Cookie detailing further facts of the story that would bring each detail to light for me.

CHAPTER 16: MORE ON THE STORY OF CHIEF RANDOLPH

Cookie's storytelling had been taking place in my living room. When we arrived back from lunch, Jewel had come in. She and Cookie spoke for a while before the account continued.

"After getting settled at my new residence, finding you, Benny, moved quickly to the top of my to-do list. I didn't know how but I had to get in touch with you quickly. By then I suspected you'd have come to mistrust my intent and therefore were avoiding me. The only person I could think of that might know how to get to you would be Garland.

"Marvin knew everybody in the city. I was confident that if I asked him, he could make contact with Garland. However, I had to act with great caution. After all,

Garland was steeped in corruption with the people now trying to kill me."

"Cookie, why would you take a chance like that?" I questioned. "Couldn't Garland have set you up; turned you over to them? What if you had run into them on your way to meeting him?" I asked, baffled by her behavior.

"I was well aware of that. I consulted with my boss and he guided me on how to handle it. I had Marvin call Garland. He found out Garland had gone for lunch at a restaurant near his work. I assumed that I could intercept him on his way back to the office.

"When I eyed him, he was walking alone. As I approached him, I could see that he was in trouble too. I knew Garland but not as well as you, Benny. Still, the demeanor of the man I saw walking down the block was not the Garland I knew. The top-of-the-world music executive looked miserable, contradicting the bright exterior he wore so naturally.

"There were lots of people out on the sidewalk. He didn't notice when I walked to his side. I tapped my finger gently on his shoulder. He nearly jumped out of his skin. He wheeled around in fright."

"Who the hell are you?" he grimaced.

"Garland—"

"He did a double take but had no idea who I was. I had purposely worn a red wool cap covering my entire head. I was dressed in a long tan coat. Over my eyes were under-sized lenses that made me look like an in-tellectual. I had thickened my eyebrows and put on fire-engine red lipstick—I didn't even know who I was when I looked in the mirror."

"How did you know how to find me?" His eyes had widened and his breathing accelerated when he no doubt recognized my voice.

"I'll explain in a moment. Just walk on ahead of me. When you get to the corner, turn left. Then the first restaurant you come to, go in and sit at a table. I'll be there in a minute," Cookie instructed.

She described a pure liquid running down his fore-head—he had to wipe it out of his eyes. "Look, I'm try-ing to—"

"Do what I tell you. I'm not here to harm you," she said reassuringly.

She wasn't surprised by his skittishness after discov-ering his association with the musical talent now under the dominion of the Parra Brothers. It had to be that they owned him as well. Any idiot watching television could figure out that in cases where organized crime was involved, it was something as simple as a short-term swing loan that couldn't be repaid timely that landed a person under the influence of the mob.

When she entered Andolini's Trattoria, Garland had done as directed. He was sitting with his head down, as if awaiting a bullet.

"I need to reach Benny Wright. It's urgent," Cookie barked at him.

"I've tried to get in touch with him myself…Cookie? What the hell are you doing?"

"I'm going to be asking the question this time, Garland. Just cooperate and I might get you out of the jam you're in."

"Benny won't return my calls."

"Garland, I know what's going on. I know about the murders—"

"I had nothing to do with any of that," Garland wept. "It was the money. I owed a fortune and I didn't have it."

"Don't dump your gambling habit on me," Cookie scoffed.

"It just got away from me. I don't know what happened," he lamented like a boy who had to recount losing a fistfight to his papa.

"I have a curiosity thing," Cookie laughed. "How much did it cost for them to buy you?"

"It was over four hundred…thousand," he sheepishly confessed.

Cookie shook her head, the sum unimaginable to a struggling investigator working case-by-case for a fee, who used to do one night gigs for fifty bucks.

"How the hell did you lose that much money?" she shoved at him. "Should have named you Charlie Brown."

"How did you know about the murder?" Garland asked, eager to move on from the subject of his addiction.

"Like I'm a damn genius. Trance was about as likely to get involved in drugs as you acting like a real person."

"I'm telling you the truth. I never imagined they'd kill him. I assumed they'd scare him and that would be the end of it."

"Well, I hope for your sake you had nothing to do with it. Garland, the same people who you're working for now are trying to find me. When they do they'll kill me. So when I leave here you're welcome to mention to them that we had a little chat. You might also tell them that I think I have a deal they might like—a trade. You call them, Garland, okay?"

"Sure," he replied tentatively.

"Now about Benny. He's in danger. I need to get to him soon."

"He promised he'd call me but hasn't. You know as much as me. The best chance is at home or Jimbo's."

Cookie stood up, leaving Garland like a bad draft.

"In my mind the man was always pathetic," Cookie sneered. "Smug, arrogant bastard who had to prove his invincibility."

"Invincibility?" I chuckled. "A Four hundred thousand dollar hit hardly sounds invincible."

"Benny, you don't get it? I didn't either until O'Keefe gave me his textbook explanation. His take was that Garland saw himself as invulnerable and engaged in acts of self-destruction to prove it."

"I still don't get it."

227

Cookie had figured out the rest of the story before O'Keefe finished. She seemed nonplussed that I could be so dense.

"You will," she laughed, eager to proceed with the telling of the tale.

Sometime later I did discuss it with my expert on abnormal behavior, Simon. He got it in a second too.

"Benny, he believes nobody and nothing can conquer him and sets out to demonstrate the point, doing unimaginably dumb things—that's the gamble. For a while he comes out like a star. The problem is that eventually the house wins. You just have to be careful to whom you're going to be accountable for your idiocy. Cookie's boss was right. His arrogance made him dumber than the average fool."

Finally, it computed in my little brain. I could then understand that when people like Garland come down from their silk perches, the earth shakes and those closest are bounced the worst.

Cookie went to Jimbo's immediately after leaving Garland. I still hadn't showed up when she arrived. Jimbo told her I'd likely drop in by the afternoon. Not wanting to panic Jewel, she was hesitant to go to my home but did try. She discovered that nobody was there. Where was I? I had taken off wandering aimlessly. I was trying to process a different dilemma, one that cropped up during the crisis three years earlier, at a time when I was attempting to glorify my family with riches. Now, I simply wanted to keep them alive.

"I planned to go back to Jimbo's in a couple hours. In the meantime, I returned to my temporary quarters to complete my work on Randolph," Cookie continued. "I called you every fifteen minutes but it was fruitless: Benny Wright had disappeared no doubt because he had convinced himself that I was working with the enemy. How was I to know you had left the phone I gave you at home?"

Cookie paused. From her expression, I'd have bet she was gloating, and she was. She had reached the subject she couldn't wait to take to the next level—the dear, Chief Randolph.

"You have to understand, Benny, that up until this phase of the journey, I was overwhelmed organizing and analyzing the masses of material being gathered by O'Keefe and myself pertaining to solving the murder of Trance—that was the priority. The personal history of Randolph I had initially approached much like a hobby, assuming it was at most a subplot that wouldn't substantially influence the bigger issue of Trance. Still, I did make a second trip to Mexico at one point to interview family members.

"Eric Randolph, Chief of Police, City of Detroit. If it were a sick joke played on the citizens of Detroit, it couldn't have been more embarrassing than it turned out. My instincts about the man were so much on target that they literally fooled me. Grab yourself a drink, Benny. Sit back and enjoy. I'm about to give you a lesson on the brilliance of the criminal mind.

"The public is generally naïve when it comes to believing how dangerous these people can be and how urgent it is for qualified authorities to be working to protect the interests and safety of the average citizen. There, I sound like a poster girl for peace officers.

"Anyway, Louis Randolph disappeared after his four-in-one performance, his slaughter of four men in the back of a truck. That explosion of violence was probably his coming out party, proving to his uncle he owned the type of sick nature needed to rise in the ranks of his organization. Indeed he did that. I was able to ascertain records documenting that he lived in Mexico. By the time Eric had graduated Yale and begun his professorship at the University of Texas, the younger Louis had earned his way up, becoming the most valued assassin and enforcer in his uncle's cartel.

"There was plenty of room for growth. Poncho, during the period he was grooming Louis, had fought many wars with competing drug gangs and withstood attacks by law enforcement personnel on both sides of the border. His drug operation was ranked number three in Mexico, and rising quickly."

As Cookie presented her lengthy expose on Eric Randolph, she showed me several documents validating the statements she was making. Incorporated in those papers were the names of two men, Raphael and En-rique Parra. They headed another Mexican drug gang, though one less prestigious than Poncho's. Nevertheless, the brothers enjoyed a close association with Poncho. In fact, the Parra Brothers were first cousins to Poncho, on his mother's side.

"These two men, The Parra Brothers, Poncho not only trusted but also admired. While Poncho and the Parra Brothers ran separate organizations, they had carved out territories distinct from each other, bound-aries they never crossed. It was known in the drug world that going to war with the Parra Brothers meant facing the full wrath of Poncho and his people, a reciprocal re-lationship that was also honored by the Parra boys.

"Poncho was known as a hothead, pothead and coke-head—he was a 'heady' guy who would typically employ all three behavior patterns at once. His thirst for power was constantly embroiling him in conflict, requiring an army of troops for the sole purpose of protecting him from the legion of enemies he was building as quickly as his empire. He was undaunted, reputed to brag ob-noxiously that there was nobody in the world that could kill him.

"He proved to be right. None of his enemies even got close to murdering him, although several tried. Poncho did them all a favor in the end. One evening while en-tertaining several select fillies from his harem, he snort-ed enough cocaine to feed his sales agents around the world for a year. The high inspired him to believe he had sprouted wings.

"At first, he clowned that he was a hawk. He ran wildly through the room with his arms outstretched, waving them to sense the air breezing past. Smiling, he'd keep passing through the ladies, taunting them as if he were about to take his mighty talons and pluck one as his prey. They all giggled—he helped them find his escapades charming by insisting they share in the bars of cocaine he had stacked up to make his dining room table look like a Dove soap factory.

"Needing to take the performance to a classic level, he dashed up to the second story of his foyer, stood on the banister over twenty feet from the marble floor, and flapped his trusty wings as he flew all of twenty feet, before slamming on the flat, cold surface.

"The report indicated his chin, which made first contact with the blue and gold colored imported marble floor, shot thousands of slivers of bone out the sides of his face like pellets from a shotgun. Blood gushed from his mouth. One of the brave witnesses to the gory scene, a recent addition to his collection of whores—she was all of fourteen, but still not the youngest—later reported to the media that she ran over to the dead body and when she tried to turn him over, noticed that his eyes, due to the extreme impact, journeyed somewhere so deep inside the head that they might have ended their trip buried in the deep structures of the brain.

"The void owing to the loss of leadership in his drug organization had to be filled, and quickly. In no time, the key officers could jump ship if they feared the cartel's collapse. At the time, Louis lacked the leadership skills, as well as the confidence of the underling officers, to take it over independently. He might have tried but surely would have failed, especially since he was plainly deficient in intellect to operate such a vast network—he had the good sense to step aside, subordinating himself to the superior management skills and years of experience possessed by the Parra Brothers.

"He had the same bond with them as his uncle. He vowed to help Raphael and Enrique in any way he could to facilitate the transition—beginning by bringing down the wrath of God on the first person that showed a sign of departing the group for another of the competitors. As the years passed, Louis showed no inclination to do anything other than loyally serve the interests of the cartel that his beloved uncle had built.

"Louis did maintain close contact with his aunts on his mother's side, but never would he ask about his brother," Cookie related in a mocking tone. "Four years ago, the Parra Brothers began looking for new channels to deal with the billions of dollars they were taking in from drug sales. They were running out of places to store the bills, which couldn't be banked conventionally—they had trucks driving around cities and warehouses throughout the world stuffed with cash that they didn't know what to do with.

"With proper payoffs, they were able to influence officials in Mexico to turn their heads as they made deposits in an institution. But it was only a tiny portion of the money. They were successful in spending some of the cash in the United States, but only in certain municipalities where they had developed relationships with local leaders who might also own small banking operations that permitted large deposits of funds. Still, this represented under ten percent of what they were holding in greenbacks—we should all have such problems," Cookie quipped. "I guess I shouldn't knock it so easily. It must be a huge problem if you consider the extent to which people go to address illegal money.

"Well, the Parra wanted their own machine, one that could convert millions, even hundreds of millions, per year. It was Mejia who had the brainstorm to use the music industry. He had worked for the Parra Brothers for years, but always as a behind the scenes consultant. He was educated in America, graduating from Cornell, and later earned a degree in finance from the Wharton School of Business.

"After spending some time in the Midwest region handling a few affairs for his employer, he approached them with his idea. They went all in. As he began to set the venture into operation, Mejia realized what he lacked most to guarantee his success...these are people who know what it takes to 'guarantee' success," Cookie poked at me, teasing about my prior experimentation with a plan going afoul that I had asserted was guaranteed.

"Thanks, darling. I'll remember that," I responded to the unflattering jibe.

"I hope you remember more than that, Mr. Wright." She waited for the intended fondness of the statements to settle with me before proceeding. "Mejia wanted not only the enforcement he knew he could provide internally. He wanted local support, mainly the police. If he had someone he could trust to look after their affairs in The Police Department, then they would be able to run the operation unchallenged."

"Louis would have been the perfect man for the job. Just buy him credentials as a police officer and let him set up his own unit," I proposed off the top of my head. "He didn't have to be chief to do what Mejia needed."

"You're correct. He didn't need the chief in his pocket but why not shoot for the moon? Besides, as far as your idea of using Louis, he couldn't even cross the border let alone fake his way in as chief."

"Then I have another idea, Cookie." I was trying to think with my criminal mind. "Why not do what every other rich group does in this country and just buy the chief?"

"That's your jaded side coming out, Benny. Not every public official is corruptible."

"No, that's not what I was saying," I smirked. "Only the ones in high level positions."

"You're being a brat. Stop it," she ordered playfully before going on with her account. "As you already know, Louis never got the job. Mejia, however, wanted to own the chief. He could have never trusted that any legitimate person serving that title would carry out the assignments he knew would be necessary to accomplish what he envisioned. No, he wanted his own chief…and he had the money to pay any price.

"Benny, the finale of Randolph is coming very soon. He's going to be a very unhappy man, I'll assure you of that," Cookie clapped her hands several times.

She could be a devilish tease—she was going to delight in making me wait for the wrap-up.

CHAPTER 17: DRESSED TO KILL

Returning now to real-time story telling, after wandering around for the day trying to figure out a plan of action, I finally came home. As it turned out, between jobs, school and after school activities, nobody had been in the house the whole day.

Jewel and my children were settling in when I came in the door. I recall it was close to five and the dark of night had just put to bed any sign of natural light. Part of my trepidation coming home was that I knew I had to tell Jewel what was happening. In fact, I had just taken her into the living room where we could talk privately, when we heard rapid banging on the door.

Jewel ran to open to see what the commotion was about. There was Cookie.

"Is Benny here?" she asked excitedly. Then as she burst into the room and when saw me seated, she harangued me. "For Christ sakes, I've come by the house several times and I've called…doesn't anyone around here answer a phone?"

"You never called me back," I shot out at her.

"What is going on?" Jewel demanded.

I understood my wife's alarm. It was as much a déjà vu for her as me witnessing a second murder. Cookie had burst into our life three years earlier and the sight of her shouting to inquire if I was home set off an unpleasant guttural reaction for my wife.

"Jewel. I'll explain on the way…" Cookie began in a pleading voice before ranting at me. "Where's the phone I gave you?"

That was when I realized I'd left it in my room. I was so embarrassed, I couldn't answer. Fortunately, she was in too big of a hurry to press the matter.

"You need to pack for a couple days for you and the kids, Jewel," Cookie ordered. "I need to get you out of here."

"Cookie, I need—"

"Jewel, please. This is about your life, Benny's and the children's. People are going to harm you, and likely kill Benny."

Hearing that late breaking news put my wife into a full sprint. While Jewel was readying us for a quick exit, I was standing alone with Cookie.

I reached into the rear pocket of my pants and took out the papers Trance had put in my car. "Trance said

I should read some papers and I'd know what to do. I had no idea what he was talking about, especially his last words when he said, 'They're in…,' but never finished the sentence.

"I'd have never found the document where he placed it in my car, had Garland not come to me cryptically suggesting that these people wanted something from me, an item I was supposed to have in my possession. That's when I thought through every detail of my contact with Trance the evening he was murdered—these papers were in the side pocket of the passenger door of my car, precisely where Trance had sat talking to me."

Waiting for Jewel, Cookie scanned the material, for the first time understanding that Trance had deputized himself to find the killers of his good friend Rough Diamond. He had to have spilled his hand and thus he was murdered. Then after the guilty parties found out he had kept a record of every detail, the search was on. Knowing I was at the murder site, they reasoned that Trance had to have given me the papers and I wasn't coming forward but held in my possession evidence that would cost the lives of some very wealthy and powerful people.

Jewel had us all packed and out of the house in fifteen minutes.

"I have a place where it's safe for us. You'll all be staying with me until this is over," Cookie explained as she hustled us into her rental car and dashed us away like a comet.

"Why would anyone want to hurt my daddy?" Shana questioned as Cookie shared more details with my wife and children.

"Because your daddy knows things that can harm other people. They're scared."

Cookie made a swift right turn, tossing all of us leftward.

"Cookie the Indy driver," my son Dion chirped. "Damn, you could get us killed and save those bad guys the trouble."

"That is some pretty heavy driving," Jewel smiled, trying to keep the tenseness of the moment light."

"Sorry. I guess I get like this when someone is trying kill me—new experience for me."

"You keep driving like this, RoboCop, and you'll get us arrested," I put in my two pennies worth. "You know what that means. Howell and his boys will haul us to a gully and—"

"Benny, will you stop it?" Jewel pleaded.

"You're right though." Cookie slowed down the car. "I want us off the streets ASAP. RoboCop?"

"Detroit, Cookie," Dion stepped in. "Don't you know the story?"

"Dion, I never had much time for fantasy in my life so why don't you give me a two-line synopsis."

"Detroit, which is supposed to be a utopia, is really just a crime-ridden city where RoboCop returns after being terminally wounded. When he comes back to the force, it's as a powerful cyborg, but with a flaw…he's haunted by memories of the past."

"Is that why I'm always wondering when I'm going to be beaten, I wonder? Sounds like my life; I'm not fooling, Dion…haunting memories? Call me Ms. Robo-Cop," Cookie exhaled her dismay.

Cookie pulled the car to a stop and jumped out. She looked carefully in all directions before motioning us to follow her. She led us around the block and then up the street. Finally, we entered into the foyer of the complex where she had rented space. We took the elevator to the fourth floor.

"Here's the rules: I don't want any of you making calls to anyone under any circumstances—those phones can be traced to this location. I don't want you to leave this suite for any reason, even for a second without my per-mission—I don't even want you stepping on the balcony. As far as the world out there is concerned, none of you exist. Jewel, I'm counting on you to make sure there are no exceptions and no compromises, understood? One mistake can cost all of your lives…and mine."

"I'm hungry," Dion moaned.

"There's plenty of food in the fridge—I stocked it up knowing I'd be having a big teenage boy staying with me, Dion," she barked at my son.

Her impatience was understandable. Cookie Acos-ta, novice investigator, was about to go to war with the Detroit Police Department's Chief and his squad of hoodlums, plus an entire drug cartel. She didn't look scared on the surface, but her sharp tongue and irritability gave her away.

"Cookie, did you study the papers I gave you?" I asked after we had settled in.

"I already figured most of it out—I know generally what it says without looking."

"How?"

"Trance Williams and I put together the same story. The only difference is that so far, I've been lucky enough to live."

"What are you going to do?" I asked.

"You'll find out tomorrow."

"I can't wait."

"No, I can't wait. Tomorrow I'll be meeting with Chief Randolph. I think he'll be very surprised I have so much to talk to him about." Cookie smiled. "Tomorrow Randolph, his henchmen, Mejia and his people, they'll all be having unexpected visitors."

That evening Jewel and I woke several times; the children were assigned the living room. Each time I checked on them, they were fast asleep. In the morning, we laid in bed, not speaking but aware we were both wishing to get the ordeal over. We never heard a sound from Cookie.

She had awakened early, planning every detail of the day so that the likelihood of mistakes was minimized.

*****

When we finally got out of bed, we showered and dressed. I left the bedroom first but Cookie was nowhere in sight and the children were still asleep. I did hear water running in the other bedroom and assumed Cookie was grooming.

The unit was in an old complex with a small but full kitchen. When I entered, I noticed a large pot of warm oatmeal on the stove. There was also a loaf of whole wheat bread and an assortment of fresh fruits as well as raisins and dried apples on the counter. A moment later, Cookie came out of the bedroom. It was eight o'clock.

I was startled by her appearance. My heart accelerated; I couldn't recognize her. I called out her name as an interrogatory and she smiled.

"I don't want anyone knowing who I am," Cookie curtsied.

Her lips were painted with a bright red balm and her face was heavily made up with wide black lines accentuating the eyebrows. She had on a wig. It was jet black with the straight hair worn in a meticulously combed pageboy cut. On top of her head was a black bowler hat.

"Did you ever see Liza Minnelli in Cabaret?" Cookie asked me as she made a partial bow.

"I did. Yeah! You look exactly like her."

"I've decided that this will be my special branding image. Whenever I have to go undercover, I'm going to take out a photo of a star I admire in a production. Then, I'll try to copy it."

"You nailed it…Liza."

"Sort of," she laughed. "My hat's a fake. I think the one she wore in the show cost three grand—I didn't want to do that to Marvin Williams."

"Thoughtful of you," I complimented.

"I'm going out soon. I have a couple of calls to make first. I'm not sure what time I'll be returning. Remind everybody about the rules."

"I'll name myself class president," I joked. "You want to tell me what you're doing?" I asked.

"Right now, I'm calling a man named Mr. Mejia—you know who he is. Before I do, let me ask you if one million dollars is enough to get you to turn over the papers. Should I make it two…or even three million?"

"If I had that much money…you might even talk me into making another run at a career in music. I still dream of it, but don't tell Jewel. It makes her feel terrible when it comes up. She feels all guilty, like she's the reason that I quit."

"I know you could have made it, Benny."

"No, you don't. That's the one thing about that industry, or for that matter anything to do with a creative pursuit. It doesn't matter how good you are, you can still fail."

"In my book, you were too good to fail."

"Thanks, Cookie. Now, in answer to your question, I'll take the three million, if you find them feeling generous."

"Let's not be greedy," Cookie countered. "It'll be one million . . . one for each of us, of course."

"What are you talking about?"

"I want to make us rich. I risk my life, I want compensation."

"Extortion?" I flustered.

"Of course. I told Mejia I'd let him know how much when I called him last night. He's waiting to hear from me," Cookie devilishly chuckled. "We're going to be rich, Benny," she exalted.

"Are you out of your mind?" I shouted, becoming more confused with each sentence of her act.

"We'll see what a million dollars does to Jewel's values. When you walk up to her with…really, two million is better—if that's okay—when you come to her with two millions dollars in hundred dollar bills in a suitcase, I wonder what that will do for that guilt."

"You're serious?" I posed in disbelief.

"No, I'm not."

"Damn it, Cookie. Do I look like I need to be teased?"

"Maybe. Now, what I'd suggest you do while I'm gone is write one of those sweet songs of yours; create one of those love ballads for Jewel. I quit and I'm okay with my decision. I was a damn good as a singer but really, where was I going to get as a back-up voice? What I'm doing now really excites me—it is who I am. But you, Benny, I'll be honest and tell you, it's pained me ever since you got out. The whole thing is different for you. You want me to guilt trip you more?"

"No. I've been down that path, Cookie. My heart's been busted too many times. You know that."

"I don't give a crap. Life is about achieving our truth. Your truth is in creation. You've learned and grown from what you went through. You'd never do something as dumb as you did before."

"That's for sure."

"If we live through this, Benny Wright, you have to promise me you'll tip-toe back in."

"I can—"

"Let me plant the seed, okay?"

Cookie picked up a small paperback book she'd been reading.

"I was saving this for the right time. I wanted you to hear it but I was hesitant to share it. It's from an author writing about artists. Ready?"

I nodded for her to proceed. What choice did I have?

> *True artists are a pathetic group of human be-ings. Against the greatest odds of success of per-haps any career endeavor, they persist. Lots of people have minds rich in intellect and pursue the study of law, medicine, physics, philosophy and a hundred other professions or disciplines. How lucky they are. If they're even decent at it, they're all but guaranteed a fair living, along with respect and recognition.*

But the artist, no matter how talented, is playing roulette with their life. If you are one, then you know what I'm talking about. They work jobs to sustain themselves, and might do it for the whole of their adult lives and never earn a thimble of currency or notoriety in their field.

There's more to the story. What makes their plight all the more afflictive is that they are powerless to travel an alternative course—they are not drawing, writing or singing of their own volition. Their soul is stamped at some point in their life and then they are sentenced for a stipulated period to expressing their inner spirit. That's how their suffering starts to come more from the perceived inability to achieve the highest level of beauty they imagine from their work as opposed to failure to be acclaimed by the public.

"Hamilton Fitz wrote it as his introduction to his book, Curses We Can't Escape. You're hurting, Benny. I've known it for the last couple of years. You can keep your soul alive and your family together at the same time. You can have it all. It's an old cliché: 'Better to have tried and failed than to have never tried,' or something like that."

"I'm going to think about it," I replied with a film of moisture covering my eyes.

"You do that. In the meantime, if anything goes wrong...if I'm not back by five this afternoon and I haven't called, then there's a problem. If by chance that happens a man named Evan Witkower will pick you up. He's an agent of the FBI, a good friend of my boss. Do not, under any circumstances, open the door unless the person uses that name. He's stationed in D. C. but flew in to Detroit yesterday. Now, if you'll excuse me, I have to call Mejia back."

"But if these people believe you're blackmailing them how will they know you won't have copied the letter and then come back for more later?" I challenged her reasoning.

"I'll give them my word."

I laughed. "Have you gone batty? These people don't believe anyone."

"That's where you're wrong. They don't have the ability to be honorable. But they do believe that people like myself can't be anything but that. They'll see my honesty as a flaw in my character. These people have checked me out. They know that I'm a simple girl with a code of honor. If I give my word, it's gold."

"Some gold," I chuckled. "You're setting them up."

"Like I told you, they think there's nothing in life but money. They're blinded by their own dogma and it's going to cost them dearly."

I heard Cookie in the other room that morning talking to Mejia. It was fairly clear she was laying down the law to power brokers that would have snuffed her out in the time it takes to blink, if she didn't have them by the testicles.

Two million in each of two separate sacks had to be

dropped in a trash container at the park. She insisted on knowing who would be making the drop off and the type of car they would be driving. She specified the precise time the money was to be left, which was ten that morning. She even warned Mejia that she wanted non-consecutive numbers on the bills.

Then she specified that she herself would be securing the delivery and if anything happened to her, the letter would be released immediately to the press and FBI where she had contacts. There was to be nobody at that park but the person leaving the money and a driver. The man responsible for dropping the money off was to get back in his car and drive away immediately. If anyone suspicious showed up in addition to the delivery person and driver, the deal was off and she intended to proceed with the alternative plan of reporting to the authorities.

Cookie stood up and walked to where there was a full-length mirror. She smiled at Lisa Minnelli.

"This might be the most famous role you've ever had," she smiled at the image reflecting the exact same mirthful look back at her.

She then came to me and leaned her lips to my cheek and kissed me. "Jewel is one lucky lady. Write a love song. Don't quit, Benny. Jewel never wanted you to stop; she only wanted you—the whole you. You'll never be whole without a lyric and a beat."

CHAPTER 18: THE TRUE STORY OF CHIEF RANDOLPH

Cookie had finalized her arrangement with Mejia. She swished out the door like a star.

I repeated the words she said to me, to write a sweet song for Jewel. Thus, while I was doing what I knew in my heart I did best, writing music, Cookie was doing what she had discovered she did best, duke it out with vicious desperados.

She had O'Keefe make a call for her the day before. She needed to get the schedule for Chief Randolph for that morning. The answer was that Randolph would be arriving at eight-thirty. He was then due to have a meeting at nine o'clock with his top officers. Cookie hated to be a spoilsport but Randolph was going to be detained.

She parked a block away and then walked to the police headquarters building. She waited until Randolph pulled into his designated spot. When she spotted him, she took out her phone and placed a call. Then, she waited for The Chief to get out of the car.

As he began walking through the lot, she approached him. She moved toward him from the side where she had sought cover behind a vehicle. He didn't recognize her in her Liza Minnelli costume. She nearly ran into him but he kept walking.

It was an unusually mild fall morning. The sun's authority was exerting itself with rays just beginning to warm the air. While Cookie was faithful to her improvisation of the great star in so far as she was wearing a black outfit, the back open and a nice breast-baring slit in the front—she wore a similar colored short skirt—she might have graduated to being a professional streetwalker.

"Chief, we need to talk," Cookie addressed him firmly.

He glanced at her, still without recognition. He kept walking at a swift pace, evidently not in the mood for the wares of a hot hooker working the police headquarters.

"You see my purse, right?" she asked. She was carrying a large leather sack, the size spoiling her outfit but a necessary tool of her trade in that she now carried a small inventory of materials when she worked. "The reason my right hand is inside my purse is because my trigger finger is wrapped around the lever of a Smith &

Weston .38 special. If I pull, you'll have bullet through your nuts."

She described Randolph as gritting his teeth so hard, he might need a dentist after their talk…if not, for sure a team of criminal lawyers.

"In case you don't recognize me, I'm Cookie Acosta. Of course, you remember meeting me some time back. I'm also the lady whose attention you've been trying to get; you know, cars towed, hoods covered with shit… but it wasn't your men who were taking shots at me that morning near The Williams home, was it?"

Randolph listened quietly.

"I want you to walk to the front of the building and then turn right. I'll be a step behind you. I'll tell you where to go from there."

Cookie instructed him to walk almost two blocks, with her reminding him all the way she was behind him with her gun ready to fire.

"I can't tell you if I were in your position what I'd do right now," Cookie contemplated on his behalf. "Would I take the bullet or the alternative, which might be at best the rest of my life in prison? Before you make up your mind, let me tell you that I have a fascinating story I want to share with you. Why don't you at least wait until after you're heard me out before deciding?"

Randolph kept walking slowly, only once glaring back at the Liza Minnelli lookalike behind him.

"You're a special case for me, Chief. I have a personal

detestation for child molesters, sadists and perverts but I don't see where you fit there. I can't say I'm fond of crooks and murderers either. I'll share with you also that it simply pisses me off when I find a person using their authority as a law enforcement official to bully, intimidate, and commit crimes including murder. Sadly, there are lots of people in each of these categories. Oh, sure, you have your place in the list of offensive acts, but when I sort it all out for you, Chief, I've found a new level of disgust—but that's what my story is about, so let's wait until we can chat comfortably, okay?"

They finally reached a narrow passageway between two buildings. The area had been landscaped with a few trees and shrubs. To the right, was a wooden bench. Cookie ordered Randolph to sit but she remained standing.

"I came by yesterday to scout out the area. That's when I found this peaceful spot. I'll bet nobody ever comes here to relax. It's not a bad place to die if you like."

"You've made a very large mistake, young lady," Randolph warned.

"No, you've made a shitload of mistakes," Cookie fired at him. "Why don't you shut up and listen. And by the way, you've never been in my shoes." She paused purposefully to see if the comment registered. "That simple statement is what set off an alarm for me. I didn't believe it. I didn't believe you. Instincts can work in magnificent ways sometimes. It wasn't just that I knew you were a lying, filthy cop, but that you, you as a person, were a cesspool of deceit."

Cookie began relating to him the history of the Randolph's family as she had researched it, as she had already shared it with me. Then, in recounting this portion of the story, she picked up right where she had left off last with me, with Mejia looking to own the Detroit Police Department.

"It was beautiful, wasn't it…do you mind if I call you Eric?" she asked, her whole presentation with the obvious intent to mock him, possibly provoke the man to force her to kill him and save the City of Detroit and the whole justice system the expense of trying a man guilty of multiple murders. "You owned a Yale pedigree, with honors. Then you became a professor. But a strange thing happened along the way, didn't it Eric? All of a sudden, your resume took a shift. You decided to attend the Buffalo Police Academy where you completed the program at the top level. You always wanting to distinguish yourself and show up that outlaw brother of yours. You then went on to the Police Training Officers program through the United States Justice Department… it's all right here in your confidential personnel file that I happened upon. Do you want to take a look?"

Randolph's skin was losing tone. He didn't reply.

"Okay then, I'll continue. After that it was off to the International Law Enforcement Academy, a Federal program that, if my memory is correct, you attended in

Budapest, Hungary…shame on me, my credentials are an embarrassment in comparison to yours. You even held a top law enforcement post after that for two years in…right, England.

"What's the point of this?" Randolph finally asked.

"I just wanted to make sure we're both starting with the same set of facts. Correct so far?"

Randolph sat mute, a murderous glint struggling to fire a death blast from his evil right eye.

"Well, I'm glad that we're in agreement. With such esteemed credentials, you were a shoe-in for Chief of this fine city. I can see why. You sailed through the interview process—with support from a few of the key city council persons you landed your first law enforcement post in the United States. You were now a respected police chief instead of a lousy professor of biological engineering. The city celebrated—I can show you the newspapers to prove it.

"You'll have to forgive me but since I sensed something foul about you, I took it upon myself to do most of the investigation of your background on my own. Every detail seemed perfectly in order and I was about to drop my suspicions about you. But then I noticed a few discrepancies in dates and a couple of other alarming facts.

"I'm a new kid at this, so I'll admit I've called for help along the way. Fortunately my boss has been around and he's been kind enough to take a special interest in helping me learn the ropes. He's a respected professor and has been called to consult on cases around the country. As a result, he has lots of close friends in law enforcement throughout America, right up to the FBI. It was with the assistance of a couple agents of that federal bureau, that I was finally able to discover the truth; the credentials of Eric Randolph were a lie.

"The man who was serving as Chief of my city had never gone to any of the programs he claimed. Would you believe it, he never served in any law enforcement role in England either? All of the records submitted to the City of Detroit had been dummied. Nobody would have detected the fraud solely from an examination of these materials. No, it would have required personal inquiries from the personnel at the esteemed schools you had reported attending. As it turned out, there was not one individual who knew of an Eric Randolph. The computer data on record at the institutions was real, but it had been corrupted to create a history that was pure fiction."

Cookie took a short break. Randolph sat quietly, shifting his posture a couple times. She waited to see if he'd lose it and leap at her.

"You know where this is going, Randolph, don't you?"

"Actually, I don't."

"You can't blame me, Eric. With all I was discovering as my investigation went on, how could I have not been curious? Even from the beginning, it baffled me why a biological scientist would want to go into law enforcement. He wouldn't, would he? No, he wouldn't.

"Now, I'll admit that I'm not sure of every detail here. I might be speculating at times, so feel free to correct me. But the way I figured it, Eric's brother, Louis, would be the one who would find it advantageous to hold an esteemed position in law enforcement, especially in Detroit. In fact, Louis might have let it be known to Mr. Mejia that he'd delight taking a stint as a Chief of Police—out of devotion for his employer…and for a little fun."

Cookie paused again. This time because she was now about to lower the boom.

"It was easy for you to kill your brother, wasn't it? You hated him. No, I can't prove it but the people in Texas might be able to. Besides, there are so many murder charges waiting to be filed against you, I think your brother will be the least of your worries.

"I'm sure you're aware that he disappeared about four years ago, just prior to when all the school transcripts and records were being generated in his name. I believe he had taken a short break—to go fishing, it seems—and he never returned. Storm. Malfunction of equipment. He just never came back. Then, since he had no family he was in contact with and only a few associates at work he was close to, there wasn't much attention paid to the event.

"It was easy for you, wasn't it, Louis? May I now call you by your true name, Louis?"

"You can call me anything you want," Randolph said quietly. "You're not shooting me in the back. If you think you have all this evidence then try to prove it. I'm leaving."

Louis Randolph stood up. Cookie leveled her gun at him. She glared as she kept the weapon pointing mortally at his heart. He turned away from her and began ambling in the direction of the street. Still she kept her aim...but...she didn't fire. As it had been planned, she didn't have to.

Randolph went about fifty feet before he neared the sidewalk. Cookie pulled back her gun and dropped the hand holding it to her side as she observed the rest of the show. As Randolph reached the end of the passageway, two men wearing suits stepped in front of him. Both held guns. One used his free hand to wave Randolph's arms in the air. He then reached to Randolph's side and took his firearm. At the other end of the walkthrough between the two buildings, two other men stood in the event they were needed.

Cookie left Randolph in the custody of the FBI agents. She had another task for that morning—she had allocated the whole day, if necessary to tie up all the loose ends she'd pulled during the course of her investigation.

Two separate packages were dropped into a trash container at Virginia Park Henry Ford off the Edsel Ford

Freeway in Detroit at precisely ten that same morning. A pair of FBI agents greeted Anthony Wilson as he deposited four million in cash in plastic bags. His partner, Roland Turner, the wheelman, was escorted out of the car and arrested by two other agents.

Cookie watched the festivities, said she wouldn't have missed it for the world. Four million. She could have deuced me and everybody else, disguised herself anew, and took off with the booty—not Cookie Acosta, no chance.

Javier Mejia was arrested at his office at exactly that moment.

The FBI was heartless. Dick Howell wasn't even allowed to finish his round of golf at the club. Saul Reyes was banging a whore at a roadside motel just outside Detroit and was about to ejaculate as the door was busted in—his erection lost its nerve, deserting the young lady.

Humberto Herrera was petting his Porsche in his garage and didn't get a chance to kiss it goodbye. Tip Owens was at home with his wife and seven year old daughter planning a trip to Hawaii—meanies wouldn't let him go.

The Parra Brothers were in Mexico at their fortress in Monterrey at ten that morning. Over three hundred officers of the FBI, Drug Enforcement Agency and Mexican police stormed the facility. Raphael and Enrique were finally arrested after a battle described as exceeding Little

Bighorn. The Parra Brothers were so heavily fortified that two attack helicopters were lost in the conflict. Officials in America knew the arrest of the brothers would do nothing to slow the trade in illegal drugs but it would send a message that there was a line not to be crossed.

Garland had already copped a deal to testify against Mejia. He may have had the crap scared out of him but he'd land on his feet, once again, "a happy cat." He did learn a lesson about accumulating debt, limiting his addiction to free cash.

That afternoon the Detroit newspapers published the astonishingly shameful and embarrassing story of… more corruption in their city.

Cookie spent the rest of the morning and the early afternoon meeting with the Mr. O'Keefe, city officials, and the FBI agents assigned to assist her. When she finished, it was about two o'clock. She had one other task to take care of before she came to release my family and me. It's what she dreaded facing the most.

She had called Marvin ahead of time ask him to round up the family at his parents' home. The only good fortune for Cookie was that the football star happened to be home for a game against his hometown Lions. Before he'd go out on the field for the game, he'd have an answer as to why his brother was murdered. He may have attained stratospheric status in the NFL but his joy would be blemished by the grief he'd experience, especially for his mom and dad.

Cookie, never having had experience dealing with bereaving loved ones of a murder victim before living with Vernon and Gloria Williams, knew that on a daily basis these proud people wept silent tears. They held their heads to the sky while their hearts sunk to the floor.

On her way to the home to meet with Trance's loved ones, Cookie wondered if the so-called experts on bereavement had it right. Would an explanation of what happened to Trance set them free to begin resolving the loss? Her common sense, contrary to the opinion of the pros, was that it wouldn't matter. She surmised that there would never be relief from the pain.

It took nearly an hour to bleed out the gory details of her investigation culminating in the mystery of why the honorable and courageous son and brother of the Williams family had been killed. When she left, she was drained. After sitting in her car crying for an hour, she headed back to the rental apartment where she had sequestered my family and me.

We were going out of our collective mind. It wasn't only the worry that something might happen to us or that Cookie might not return. Added to that was pure boredom. The children couldn't get on the internet and we had no board games to play. We'd been instructed to not even go outdoors. The television was all we had and since there was only one, Dion and Shana spent most of the day bickering.

When Cookie finally arrived, she looked weary.

"Did you write the song?" she darted at me like an accusation.

"Matter a fact, I did," I answered her.

"Good. You're all free to leave now. Call me in a week and wake me up, will you?"

She smiled and then walked to the bedroom and closed the door.

That was it. Two innocent and decent kids with a wonderful future killed for no reason other than having honor and integrity. Even after the arrests and later convictions, the families and friends of Trance Williams and Brent Calhoun would never be relieved of suffering. But these two were only a sample from a much larger pool of wonderful people whose lives have been cut short due to crime, particularly drug-related, and senseless violence.

I didn't attempt to find an answer that would stop the killing...there was none and never would be. Man has the unfortunate capacity to behave savagely and unless he lives in the heart of the universal oneness where he finds love, he will make an occupation using fear and greed to betray his fellow man—and we are the highest order of living species?

THE END

OTHER NOVELS COMPLETED AND UPCOMING BY

Dennis A Nehamen

Mistaken Enemy

Insatiable Hate

Mescalero Blood

Crushing Steel

Musicball

DOGMAi

The Making of A Madman

Misty's Place

The Greatest American Outlaw

Crushing Dreams

Juliette

ABOUT THE AUTHOR

Dennis A Nehamen, Ph.D. is a forensic and clinical psychologist who has authored novels, screenplays and mu-
sicals, including the award-winning musical *Wrapped*.
He lives in Los Angeles with his wife and has two adult
children.